The Diary of a Side Chick 4

A Naptown Hood Drama

Tamicka Higgins

© 2015

D1359804

Disclaime

This is a work of fiction. Names, places, characters and events are all fictitious for the reader's pleasure. Any similarities to real people, places, events, living or dead are all coincidental.

This book contains sexually explicit content that is intended for ADULTS ONLY (+18)

Chapter 1

Desirae was actually starting to feel proud of how she was handling things, despite everything that had been going on in the last couple of weeks between her and Tron, not to mention the falling out with Reese. She was getting used to this being pregnant thing. In fact, she no longer craved smoking a blunt the way she did before. A glass or two of wine? She did not need or want that either. Rather, every morning, when she would wake up and look at herself in the mirror and see how her body was slowly but surely changing, everything that she did was for the best interest of her unborn child. There were moments, however, that she wished Tron would do the same – think about the best interest of the baby and do things differently.

After working with her mother to get back onto her health insurance, Desirae just so happened to wind up getting her first doctor's appointment on February 14th – Valentine's Day. She remembered how she shook her head when she was on the phone, calling the office to set up an appointment. While she and Tron were never actually together on a Valentine's Day, the very thought of going to the doctor on that kind of day did make her feel some kind of way. Nevertheless, when she woke up that morning, now getting used to lying on her back as she slept, she rubbed her stomach. Desirae, out of instinct from knowing that she was a strong woman, would rub her stomach before she slid her legs off the bed and onto the floor. There, she would sit for a few minutes. Some mornings she felt alright, while other mornings she would sit and then the feeling would come over her – the feeling that she was about to throw up and needed to rush to the bathroom as quickly as possible.

Today, February 14th, Desirae woke up and was actually feeling okay. While much of her situation was still uncertain, mainly because she no longer was working at Clarke's up at Lafayette Square Mall, she still felt as if she was heading somewhere. She admitted to herself that she sort of missed the job, even if her only reason for missing it was for the consistent paycheck and relatively easy workload that she had. That was all behind her at this point. Now, she has to look forward – move on. And she was going to try to make the best of it, regardless of her feelings.

Desirae slid into her robe and got officially under way with getting her day started. Out of instinct, as she always did, she grabbed her phone off of the pile of her clothes on the floor next to her bed. She checked to see if she had any text messages or missed phone calls. A number had called in the middle of the night that she was not familiar with. She shrugged it off, thinking it was probably just another wrong number. In her text messages, she saw that Reese had messaged her around 1 a.m., which was shortly after Desirae remembered going to sleep.

"Fuckin' bitch," Desirae said to herself. She shook her head and sat her phone back down, this time onto her bed. Never in all of her life had she known what it felt like to really be betrayed. Sure, on one hand Tron truly had done her dirty. How he treated her was absolutely inexcusable, and Desirae, deep down, was not totally passed that anyway. However, walking into the club and seeing her very best friend, Reese, was a fucking blow to her system. Never had she felt as angry as she did when she thought about all of the things she had confided in Reese about. To turn around and find that she would try to walk a mile in her shoes was just disgusting.

Disgusted with that thought, Desirae dropped her phone onto the bed. Just as she was starting to stretch and open her blinds to let some of the morning light inside, she could hear her phone vibrating. Quickly, she picked it up and saw that it was her mother calling. While Desirae and her mother, Karen, were definitely different kinds of women, Desirae could not deny how appreciative she was that her mother was being so helpful with her pregnancy. It was a blessing that she was about to get onto her health insurance and use it while she was pregnant, with her mother paying whatever would be the difference for adding her onto the plan.

"Hey, Mama," Desirae answered, smiling.

4

"Well, good orning, Desirae," her mother Karen said, clearly sounding as if she was smiling. "How are you this morning? How are you feeling? You sound like you're in a good mood, Desirae."

"I am," Desirae said. "I just got outta bed and was getting ready to start getting ready and stuff. Bout to look at what I'm gonna wear to the doctor's office."

"Well," Karen said. "You don't have to go trying to look cute to go to your first doctor's appointment for this baby. You're not going in there to catch a man. You know that, right?"

Desirae let out a deep sigh, shaking her head. She then rolled her eyes and smiled. "Mama," she began, "I don't know why you just can't get on board with how I dress. You wanna be young again so bad, don't you? C'mon now, why don't you just say it?" Desirae giggled.

"Girl," Karen said, snickering to herself. "I'm more than twice your age and three times as cool as you. You can't talk. Anyway…"

"Yeah, right," Desirae said. "Yeah, I go down there at 11 o'clock."

"That's what I was going to ask you," Karen said. "I was just thinking of that because I forgot what time you were going. I just got to my desk, myself. So, I thought I would call you. Don't forget what I told you. I can take my lunch at that time if you tell me enough in advance that you want somebody to go with you since this is your very first appointment. I can do that and it wouldn't be a problem."

"Thanks, Mama," Desirae said. "But I'mma go on my own. I think I just need to do this on my own."

"Okay," Karen said. "No problem." Karen paused. The sound of her typing on the keyboard of her computer at work came through the phone for a few seconds. "I always wanted to ask: Did you ask the father if he would like to go? This Tron person I've been hearing about for about a month, who is having a child with my daughter, and I still have not met. Did you ask him if he would want to go? Sometimes a man just wants to be included, and he should be given that right. In all my years of teaching and social work, I can definitely tell you

5

this: too many of these mothers purposely try to keep the father away. Don't be that woman, Desirae. I swear, not only will you live to regret it, but when your child gets older and either learns the ways of the world or begins to have a relationship with his or her father, you then have to worry about them learning what mama did back when they were younger."

Desirae thought about what her mother was saying to her right then. She stood at her window, feeling hugged by her favorite robe – the white robe – that she still looked good in. Beams of light came in through the blinds as she looked out at the parking lot of her apartment complex. The tops of cars and trucks were covered in snow while the wooded area that was behind the apartment complex was simply a white-washed winter wonderland. Desirae turned away and walked out into her living room.

"Yeah, I talked to him, Mama," Desirae said. "He said he didn't want to go, so I'mma just go on my own. Something about he had something to do that day, or something."

Desirae had practically had this story already prepared, in a way. She had kind of thought that her mother would ask about Tron and if he would be going to the doctor's appointment. After she went to jail for aggravated assault, luckily Tron didn't press charges and the judge decided to let her free because she could prove that she was pregnant, Desirae had called her mother back after two days of not talking to her with a story about something being wrong with her phone and that she was sick. Her mother bought that, no problem, which Desirae was so happy about. She knew that she would never hear the end of it if her mother knew what all happened at Honeys East. Now, with the idea of Tron going to the doctor with her, she had never even sent so much as a text message to him about it. At this point, it was really none of his business.

"Yeah, he's busy or something," Desirae said. "And, Mama, like I told you, we really not together."

"And?" Karen said. "That still doesn't mean that he doesn't want to be involved. Also, when are you moving back in over here? When are you planning to move out of your apartment, again, so I can be prepared for that? I looked in the garage and looked at where you could put your stuff until you're back on your feet and found a new job and whatnot. I think it can work so you don't have to spend money on a storage unit. Plus, we got the basement, so you can put stuff down there. I don't care."

"In about a week, Mama," Desirae answered. She walked across her living room and into the kitchen to get something to drink. She poured herself a glass of tea and leaned against the counter. For whatever reason, with where she was standing, she could not help but to think about the times Tron would lean against the counter, in this very spot, and lean back while Desirae was on her knees and pleasing him in ways that his chick Shawna obviously never could. Quickly, because she was talking to her mother, she put those thoughts out of her mind. "The landlord lady down at the office said that I could move out on Friday, depending on the weather."

"Okay then," Karen said to Desirae. "I can be free to help you. What about Reese? You think she can help you? She helped you move into the apartment back whenever, didn't she?"

Desirae cringed. In many ways, she felt as if she wanted to scream at just hearing someone say Reese's name. In fact, her emotions reacted to the very thought of Reese way differently than they had when she thought about her in her bedroom. Without even thinking, Desirae's eyes slanted to the side as she sipped her tea.

"No, Mama," Desirae said. "I told you that me and Reese ain't cool no more." Desirae's head shook. "Nope," she said. "I don't want nothin' to do with her, Mama."

"Hmm, hmm," Karen said, in a very flat tone. "Interesting. I wonder what happened there."

Desirae stood silent, choosing to not say anything. She remembered that she had already told her mother that she simply was not going to talk about why she and Reese had had a falling out. It was not that she did not want her mother to know why, per se. However, Desirae also knew that with the way her mother analyzed stories and situations, she would find any little hole in the story. And these holes would be stretched to the point where her mother would figure out that something went down that night that had Desirae facing charges.

"Okay, well," Karen said, knowing that she was not going to get anything else out of her daughter. "I better go on and get to work. I've got to head down to the south side to meet with this family – trashy white people. You know how that is. Text me or call me or whatever when you get back and let me know how it all went."

"Okay, Mama," Desirae said. "I will. Talk to you later."

The two of them said bye and hung up. Desirae then set her phone on the counter and headed to the bathroom. Sitting her cup of tea onto the counter of her bathroom sink, she opened her robe. Desirae faced the mirror and took a good look at her body. Her shape was still definitely killing the scene, as she knew when she went downtown a couple of days ago and had men still losing their minds to look at her when she walked by. However, as the days went on, she spent a few moments of every morning looking at her reflection in the mirror. She was now getting to the point where she could see her stomach starting to stick out a little further than it used to – having a round look that had PREGNANT written all over it. The one thing she was definitely excited about, with going to the doctor for the first time, was finding out how many months along she was. She also looked forward to knowing her due date, remembering that sometimes that would be her favorite part about her friends having their babies.

"I'm still gon' look good," Desirae said to herself as she turned side to side in front of her bathroom mirror. "I'm not gon' be one of them raggedy, tired pregnant chicks that you see walking around, looking like they need to get their life." Desirae already had maternity clothes ideas that she knew would turn into cute outfits. For now, though, she could continue to wear her normal clothes and not look pregnant, especially since she walked around covered up in a coat because it was the middle of February.

After a brief few minutes of looking at her body in the mirror, Desirae turned on the shower, to a really nice, warm temperature, and climbed in. For the next twenty minutes, she cleaned every part of her body as she sang songs that she had heard on the radio yesterday. When she got out of the shower, she wrapped a towel around her body and walked back out to her phone on the counter in the kitchen.

"Fuck, it is cold as shit out here," Desirae said to herself, shivering. She checked the time and saw that she had better go ahead and start getting ready. There was a good chance that she might have to scrape some ice off of her car and let it warm up for a few minutes before she could head up to the north side, to where her doctor's office was located. She turned the television on, waiting until the news butted in with weather updates about the day, then decided what she would wear. She slid into some cute blue jeans, a black sweater that had the perfect turtle neck, then a leather jacket that her mother had given her as a present just a couple of Christmases ago. She brushed the arms of the jacket before she looked over her hair and got it together. When she knew that she was looking good, Desirae grabbed her purse and phone and headed out the door.

Desirae sat in her car for a few minutes while it warmed up. The temperature was kind of cold today, but the sun was out, so that made a difference. When she turned on the radio, she could not help but to think about how it was Valentine's Day. The DJs on the radio stations let people call in and give shout-outs to whoever is their "Valentine," then some callers could request a song. Soon enough, Desirae had just heard enough of all of that love mess. She turned the radio off, the silence now leaving her to think about how she was single and carrying some nigga's child, who never had any intentions of being serious with her like she had said. Desirae pressed her lips together as she backed out of her parking spot, thankful that she did not need to scrape any ice off of her windshield, windows, and mirror. She headed out to the stop light and turned left, heading toward the interstate.

It took Desirae about twenty-five minutes to get across town to her doctor's office. The office, which was located in a little subdivision of offices that surrounded a retention pond, was on the opposite side of the city, near Castleton Mall. When she pulled into a parking spot outside of the glass doors of the mid-rise brick building, she saw that she had an extra thirty minutes to kill before she even needed to head into the building. To kill time, she pulled her phone out of her pocket and looked through her messages. After responding to a couple of text conversations with her cousins that she had left open, forgetting to go back and respond if she would be at the next family function or not, she found herself scrolling through her conversations with Tron. Her feelings were mixed, for many reasons, as she could see that there had been no communication from him since he declined to press charges on her from the incident at Honeys East. She was so enraged that not that even to this day, she could not and would not regret that. Her entire life was basically changing before her eyes because of Tron. How could he not at least give her the time of day and the respect that she knew she deserved?

Desirae got out of her car around 10:50 and headed into the building. She felt a little nervous, but also a little excited. Once inside, however, her mind could not help but focus on what she saw around the office. After signing in and letting them know that she was there, Desirae sat down in the small waiting room. She noticed that other women, who looked to be a little older than her, but not by much, were sitting next to men – men who were either their husband or the father of the child. After a few minutes, Desirae could not stand to look around the room and see this. Even though she had never really been big on dreaming about weddings and whatnot like a lot of other girls, now that she was pregnant she started to notice more and more when she would see another chick with the father present. It really sunk in on her when the chick was the same age as her, and even more-so when the chick did not look half as good. Part of her, even though she did not want to admit it, felt like if the Plain Janes could have it, then she damn sure should have it.

Within minutes, a plump, smiling white girl yanked open the door to the back and yelled Desirae's name. Desirae instantly stood up and smiled as she walked over to the door.

The nurse, whose name tag said Becky, welcomed Desirae and told her that Doctor Adair is ready for her to come on back. Desirae stepped into the back where the nurse asked her some questions and weighed her.

"Congratulations," the nurse said to Desirae.

Desirae smiled, looking down at her stomach. "Thank you," she said.

"Will this be your first?" the nurse asked.

Desirae nodded. "Yeah," she answered.

Becky smiled. "I remember my first," she said. "I remember when me and my husband went to the doctor appointments and how exciting it was to find out different things."

Desirae glanced at the floor with hearing the word *husband*. "Yeah," she said when she looked back up. "I am excited to find out stuff. I'm a little scared and nervous."

Becky patted Desirae on the shoulder and smiled. "Don't be," she advised, in a loving way. "There is nothing to be scared of. Pregnancy can be a wonderful thing...it really can."

"Yeah," Desirae said, sounding unsure of that part. She imagined herself giving birth, putting her face in the scene like she had seen on television shows and in movies. "I am not looking forward to the actual giving birth part."

"Yeah," Becky said, nodding her head as she began to take Desirae's blood pressure. "That's the part that definitely kinda sucks." Becky giggled. "But, it all really depends."

Desirae looked up into Becky's face, feeling content with the fact that this nurse was nice and that for the first time in some days she felt like she could talk to someone about something. It was even better that this woman was a stranger and did not know anything about Desirae that Desirae did not want her to know. "Can I ask you something?" Desirae said.

Becky looked at her and smiled. "Sure," she said.

"This labor thing," Becky said. "How bad is that really?"

Becky sucked air in through her teeth. "Well," she said, as she was clearly trying to find the perfect words to describe it. "It really depends on the woman, and probably how many children she has already had. Typically, your first child will be

11

the hardest because you've never done this before. However, that does not happen to everybody."

"What's the longest anyone has ever been in labor, that you know of?" Desirae asked.

Becky took a moment to think about it. "I remember a lady, before I moved here, back in South Bend, who was in labor for like three days," she answered. "Now, that was pretty intense. I went home from work and came back like two days in a row and she was still there, but no baby!" Becky laughed. "Poor thing."

Desirae's head shook. "God, I hope that ain't me."

Just then, Doctor Adair walked into the room. The doctor was a somewhat tall black woman. To Desirae, she resembled the actress Angela Basset in a lot of ways. Her mannerisms were especially similar. Soon enough, Desirae could hear the doctor talking with an East Coast accent.

The doctor introduced herself to Desirae, who loved seeing that the doctor was a mature black woman. When Becky finished up doing her nursing duties, she slid out of the room.

"Are you excited, Desirae?" Doctor Adair asked with a professional smile.

"Yeah," Desirae answered. "I am now."

Doctor Adair looked at Desirae with a plain face, but was sizing her story up based on how she was dressed and how she talked. "Well," she said. "That is good."

After the doctor got some necessary information from Desirae, she walked her down to the x-ray and ultrasound room. Realty really sunk in when the nurse came into the room and began to rub the gel on her stomach. She had always seen this sort of thing on television, but never dreamed in a million years that she would be starring in such a role. Soon enough, the doctor was telling Desirae how many months along she was with her pregnancy.

"Well," Doctor Adair said. "Miss Desirae, it definitely looks like you are three months, or twelve weeks, pregnant."

Desirae was shocked to hear that, considering that she had not really gained much weight, if any at all. "Oh, okay," Desirae said, smiling. She counted six months into the future in her head, figuring that she would be having her baby sometime in either August or September – a fall baby.

"But that's not all," the doctor said as she looked at the computer and other information. "Miss Desirae, you are pregnant with twins."

Desirae's eyes damn near popped out of her sockets hearing something like that. The words *pregnant with twins* echoed in her mind. Since finding out that she was carrying Tron's baby, Desirae had already mentally prepared herself for the idea of taking care of one child. Never in a million years did she think a doctor would tell her that she is pregnant with twins. Part of her wanted to be excited, as she was not totally opposed to the idea of having two children. However, another part of her – the part of her whose voice was so loud that it could not be overlooked or ignored – was scared shitless. Maybe *terrified* would be a better word, because she was already starting to feel the pinch of adulthood that came with taking care of herself in a world that was so cold. Taking care of one baby was going to be a challenge – two babies sounded like a fucking beautiful nightmare.

"I'm pregnant with twins?" Desirae asked Doctor Adair, clearly surprised.

Doctor Adair remained stern and professional, but smiled as she sent the ultrasound to a printer so that Desirae could take a copy home. "Yes, you are," she answered. The doctor was not the least bit surprised at Desirae's response. Having twins was generally a shock for any woman, regardless of her age. However, the doctor had seen throughout her career that the younger the woman, the bigger the reaction. Based on how Desirae spoke and some of her mannerisms, Doctor Adair got the vibe that this girl was neither educated nor in a committed relationship. "I know this may be hard to hear," she said. "But I need for you to not stress too much over this. Like I said, I know it must be hard not to, but stress is not going to do you any good in this situation."

"Twins, though?" Desirae said. Her emotions were now taking over as she was thinking about what having twins would mean for her life. "Are you serious?"

13

Doctor Adair pointed at the screen and said frankly, "These are two bodies, Desirae. You are twelve or so weeks in, and you are having twins. It is too early to see the sex, because that mostly can't be seen until around week eighteen or nineteen, sometimes as early was week seventeen. However, I can definitely see here that you are having twins."

Desirae looked down at the floor, knowing that whatever plans she had thought up for getting her life back on track and taking care of a baby would now have to change. Part of her thought that she was going to be able to do this without ever calling on Tron and asking him for anything. That, however, was looking as if it was going to be different. There was just no way that she was going to be able to take care of two babies on her own.

"I can't believe this," Desirae said.

Doctor Adair looked at Desirae, seeing the mental anguish in the young woman's face. Badly, she wanted to ask Desirae about her situation. Where was the father? Why did he not come with her? Sure, the doctor had black couples come to see her all the time. However, she could not deny for one minute that an overwhelming majority of single women who came to see her were black. Nonetheless, she remained silent and allowed Desirae to sort through her feelings.

***

When Desirae left Doctor Adair's office with so much new information to process, she stepped off of the curb of the sidewalk just outside of the building doorway without looking. Quickly, a car swerved, honking its horn as it avoided hitting her. Jumping back, she realized how zoned out with disbelief she was, pulled herself together, and walked across the parking lot. For the entire walk, which seemed twice as long as the time it took her to head into the building when she got there, the words *pregnant with twins* were all she could think about. For whatever reason, she felt like she had been cursed in a way she did not deserve. She knew that her life was about to become twice as hard as she had originally planned. And her situation was even worse because these twins had a father that was some nigga who refused to live up to his word.

14

When Desirae got into her car, she immediately turned the heat on. She had begun to pull out of the parking spot when she simply stopped the car and remained parked. Zoning out on the traffic rushing down 96th Street, she leaned her head back into the headrest and turned the radio down. In silence, she could hear her heart beat. Occasionally, the sound of squawking geese flew over in the skies above the office plaza.

"I don't fuckin' believe this," Desirae said, shaking her head. "Twins? Twins? This can't be happening." She knew that it was. Her eyes saw just what the doctor's eyes had seen. There indeed did appear to be two little bodies inside of her. Everything began to get so serious. She would have to deal with Tron, who she knew would not respect her, especially after she let him have it with that fork. Then, on top of that, she had no choice but to let her best friend Reese go. She would never be able to trust her again after she was clearly up at Honeys East that night to see what Desirae had been getting. Desirae thought about how if she were still friends with Reese, this mind be easier to handle. However, this was simply not the case.

Once Desirae calmed down, she pulled her phone out of her pocket and texted her mother: *Just left the doctor...Twins.*

Not even believing it as she texted the words, Desirae dropped her phone into the drink holder and went back to leaning her head against the seat. Within seconds, she could hear her phone vibrating again. She had immediately assumed that it was her mother either responding to the text or calling back. Desirae quickly grabbed her phone and found that it was not her mother. Rather, a text message had just showed up from Reese. "What this bitch want?" Desirae said to herself, her nostrils flaring as she opened to the text message.

Reese: *Can we talk?*

Desirae looked side to side for a minute, hating that she even still had Reese's phone number saved in her phone. She wondered why she had not already deleted it since she was done with Reese for good. At this point, however, there was nothing to hold Desirae back from letting Reese know how she felt. She needed to let off some of her frustration anyway. Who better to get it than the very person who had betrayed her the most?

Desirae: *What the fuck you want?*

Desirae smirked as she hit SEND on that text message. Within seconds, her phone was vibrating with Reese calling her. As soon as Desirae answered, she could hear Reese putting on that sweet, innocent voice that had fooled her for so long, evidently.

"Bitch, what the fuck you want?" Desirae asked coldly as she answered the phone. "Why the fuck you callin' me? Ain't you got some dick out there that don't belong to you that you supposed to be chasin'?"

"Desirae," Reese said. "You know it wasn't even like that. I know you seen me try'na call you and stuff since you went up to that club and stabbed Tron."

"It wasn't like that?" Desirae asked. "Bitch! What the fuck do you mean it wasn't like that? I know what I saw and you was up there try'na get with the father of my fuckin' child like some desperate ass THOT out here. I don't even know why you try'na cover that up, and I don't know why the fuck you would even be callin' me thinkin' that we gon ever, ever, ever be cool like we was again, bitch. Who the fuck do you think I am and shit?"

"Desirae," Reese said in a pleading voice. "You just assumed, but I was really up there to see what he was doing so that I could tell you."

Desirae was not even trying to hear Reese make any sort of excuses for why she was up there. She was so disgusted that Reese could even have the audacity – the balls – to come calling her and thinking that she could smooth everything over.

"Bitch," Desirae said. "I know why you was up there. And I only answered the phone so I could let your no good ass know where the fuck to get off. You was up there try'na get with Tron, who you knew was talkin' to me. Guess you just really had to try some of the dick, huh? You probably done

16

been back up there and on your knees to try to get him to like your old dusty ass."

"Dusty?" Reese said, now feeling insulted. Sure, she felt guilty about even for one second thinking of popping into Honeys East. While she never actually did get to the point of doing anything with Tron, she was as good as guilty already, at least in the court of public opinion. "Desirae, I really don't think you the one who need to be callin' anyone names. You was just that nigga's hoe, then you get mad and always gotta talk my ear off about how he treat you like a hoe."

"Hoe?" Desirae said, now really mad. "I swear to God, Reese. I don't wanna ever see you in life again. You lucky I'm pregnant or else I'd find your ole tired, no butt, no titty havin' ass and beat that ass like it obviously need to be beat. You lucky them niggas up at the club pulled me off that ass, cause you know I was about to tear it up, don't you? You know I was about to beat that ass somethin' fierce. Girl, I woulda dragged you around that floor and out the door and embarrassed that ass and you know it."

"Whatever, Desirae," Reese said. "You know you overactin' and shit."

Desirae had had enough at this point. She knew that her former best friend must have been one crazy bitch to even come calling and trying to cover up her tracks. Desirae did not care if Reese actually got to do anything with Tron or not. The fact that she was somewhere she had no business being was enough for her.

"I swear to God, bitch," Desirae said. "As soon as I drop these fuckin' babies, I'mma come beat that ass. After that, I swear to God I don't wanna ever see you again in life."

"Babies?" Reese asked, sounding surprised. "That nigga got you pregnant with twins?"

Desirae shook her head, hating that she even answered the phone. "Bitch, bye," she said then ended the call. Nostrils flaring and her hormones raging just a little bit too much, Desirae tossed her phone into the front passenger seat. Within seconds, it was vibrating again. However, she was in no mood to answer, already knowing that it was Reese calling her back. The level of betrayal that Desirae felt from that chick was just something she could not overlook, and she never would.

Desirae pulled out of her parking spot and headed toward the busy 96th Street. As she got out into the road and headed toward the highway, she slowly put Reese out of her mind. Soon enough, she was contemplating how she was going to approach the situation with Tron. How would she tell him that she was pregnant with two babies? She hated that she was going to have to play her cards right just to have some help with her situation. While she would have to tell him soon, she would also have to work on moving out of her apartment and in with her mother. Her life was just changing so much, so quickly.

Chapter 2

February 14th. Valentine's Day. For the last couple of days, Shawna had actually been rather busy. Usually, with the kind of snow and ice that was typical of winters in Indiana, especially during late January and early February, her appointments would decrease. This year, however, things had been rather good – not necessarily as busy as they might be on a spring, summer, or fall day, but surely more clients were getting their hair done than usual. While this was certainly good for Shawna, it came with a price. As each woman came in to have her hair done, she basically spilled her guts about the plans she had for Valentine's Day.

These conversations only served as reminders of what Shawna had lost. In a matter of days she went from being happily in love with Tron to being so mad at him that she could feel her blood pressure rising from just thinking about it. In fact, there were days when she would be chilling at her sister Morgan's place that Shawna would have to just sit down and think. She felt so embarrassed at the thought of even trying to work anything out with Tron. Not only did he have a side chick, and was going to meet her when he was supposed to be out of town, not to mention lying about it when Morgan had seen him, but the side chick was also pregnant. There are certain things that Shawna would like to think that she could look past. However, staying with a man that gets his side chick pregnant is simply not one of them. Now, more than ever, Shawna wanted to do whatever needed to be done so that she could push through and move on.

Now, with it being Valentine's Day, and having to listen to days and days of clients' plans for the day, Shawna woke up and spent this February morning chilling on the couch. Sometimes she actually watched a show, and other times the television was simply on. It acted as background noise to what she was thinking. This Valentine's Day was the first in many years that she had been alone. And it came on the heels of the fall of their relationship, not to mention that nigga basically making a fool out of her.

"Fuck him," Shawna said. She sipped on a glass of cranberry juice while she lounged about, sprawled across her sister Morgan's couch. Still, after being here for basically two weeks and some change, she was not used to it. She felt like she was so above this – above having to stay with a friend because of what went on in her relationship. There were days that she regretted getting her stuff together and moving out of the townhouse. However, that was now water under the bridge. She had been gone too long to go back. And going back would probably only remind her of the betrayal even more, not to mention the mental anguish that would come at this point from trying to get Tron to move out.

Shawna checked her cell phone, looking at the time. It was approaching noon. She glanced out of the window, at the snow-covered car roofs in the parking lot of Morgan's apartment. She then looked around the apartment, noticing yet again how Morgan's furniture and layout was nowhere close to what she had with Tron. Never did she think her lifestyle – or quality of life – would change so quickly.

"I'm good," she said to herself. "I got two hours before I gotta get ready to head to the shop and do Ms. Susan's hair." *That's my girl*, Shawna thought.

When Shawna had gotten up this morning, her sister Morgan was in her room getting ready to go to breakfast with her boyfriend, Chris. Shawna did have to admit to herself that it was kind of nice that she and her sister's roles in their sisterly relationship had changed. For quite some time, it had been Morgan giving Shawna relationship advice – giving her advice whether she wanted it or not. With the tables turning, Shawna now got a chance to look at her sister's love life. And she loved making comments, even thought of it as getting even for some of the things Morgan would say to her when she was living with Tron.

Just as Shawna snickered under her breath and sipped her orange juice, she heard keys outside of the apartment door. It was Morgan coming back from breakfast. Quickly, Shawna jumped up off of the couch and rushed over to the door to unlock it.

"Girl, thank you," Morgan said as she stepped in then pushed the door shut. "It is so cold out there."

20

"Yeah," Shawna said, heading back to the couch. She then looked over at Morgan, who was taking her coat off and throwing it onto the counter that looked into the kitchen. Morgan was smiling ear to ear, making Shawna wonder why she was so damn happy. "What the hell is up with you?" Shawna asked. "Wait a minute… It's like noon or something, I think. Why you back from breakfast so fast? Did they put y'all out because they switched over to lunch?"

Morgan rolled her eyes, still smiling, as she went back to her bedroom. She took her shoes off and changed out of her black dress and into some gray sweatpants and an old t-shirt.

"I told you, Shawna," Morgan said when she came back into the room and slumped down into the couch, next to Shawna. "We was just going to breakfast because he has to be at work later. You know that Valentine's Day ain't no national holiday or nothing."

Shawna chuckled. "With how you smilin', I would have thought that it was," she said, looking at her sister with questioning eyes."

"Stop hatin', Shawna," Morgan said.

"I ain't hatin'," Shawna said. "I'm just observing…and something is up with you. I can tell. I don't know why you just don't go ahead and tell me. Cause you know you want to tell me anyway, so just go ahead and spill it, girl. What did y'all do after, or before, breakfast?" Shawna leaned in and smiled. "Did y'all fuck for the first time?"

"Girl, boo," Morgan said, shrugging her shoulders. She was still smiling, shaking her head from side to side. "We done been done that."

"Awe," Shawna said, very surprised at what she had just heard. She playfully slapped her sister on the shoulder. "You hoe! You ain't even known him for three solid months, if that, and you done already fucked?"

Morgan looked at Shawna, clearly wanting to know how she could say anything. "And how soon was you lettin' Tron up in you?" she asked. "Huh? Tell me that."

Shawna looked away. "We ain't talkin' bout me," she said. "So, um, anyway, how was breakfast?"

Just then, Morgan held up her hand, showing Shawna a ring on her first finger, left hand. Out of the corner of her eye, Shawna noticed something shiny and silver on her sister's hand. She turned and looked, zooming her attention in on the ring.

"What the fuck is that?" Shawna asked. "What is that, Morgan?"

Morgan turned the top of her hand toward her face and fidgeted her fingers, clearly admiring the ring. "What does it look like?"

"I know what it looks like," Shawna said. "I'm asking you what it is? What is that, Morgan? What kinda ring is that?"

"You know what kind of ring it is, Shawna," Morgan said.

"No," Shawna said, shaking her head. "This don't make no sense. I don't even remember you mentioning that you knew him around Christmas, if not New Years. And now, it's Valentine's Day, and I still ain't met this nigga, and he done put a ring on it?"

Morgan nodded, still smiling. "Basically, girl," she said. "Ain't it nice?" She held her hand toward Shawna, allowing her to grab her hand and have a closer look.

Shawna, in disbelief at what she was seeing and hearing, lightly held her sister's hand. She looked up and into Morgan's face. "Girl," she said. "Are you crazy or something? You ain't known this nigga for nothing but a minute, Morgan. And now he done actually proposed?"

"He's the one, Shawna," Morgan said. "I know it. I didn't even care what the ring looked like. You know we been spendin' so much time together. He got a new job offer and is going to have to move away. But he said that there is no way that he can go without me. So, we was out to breakfast, girl, at this nice restaurant downtown with a bunch of rich white people, you know. And we was talkin' about us and everything."

22

"Wait a minute," Shawna said, confused for days. "Tell me this, first. How did he propose to you if the job was based on you going or not?"

"Well," Morgan said, not being able to wipe away the excitement from her face. "He told me about the job, and I started to get real sad, you know. You finally find someone and you can tell that it is the real thing. I mean, we really got love for each other. That's what makes this different, Shawna. I never loved a dude like I love him. Everything about us goes together. We stay on the phone, texting or talking. I like his family and he got a good job and stuff."

"Okay, okay," Shawna said, shaking her head. "So he tells you that he got a job offer? Where?"

"Chicago," Morgan answered. "And girl, you know we gon' be livin' on the nice side of Chicago, not on the side where you see all that stuff on the news... Chiraq or whatever they call it. He gon' be makin' some real money now, and you know, I can get into some things in Chicago that can make some money." Morgan looked down at the ring when she took a pause from explaining. "So, yeah, we was out to breakfast and he told me about the job. I thought it was going to be like him breaking up with me or something. I was getting' all sad and shit, emotional, you know. Then, next thing I know, I am puttin' syrup on my pancakes and he is tellin' me that he will only take the job if I agreed to go with him ... If I would agree to go with him."

"Okay," Shawna said, understanding that part. "So, how do we get to the ring part? How did you wind up with this on your finger?"

"You know my rule, girl," Morgan said. "I ain't movin' away with no man unless he put a ring on it first, then we can talk. I guess he knew I was that kind of chick because after we talked about whether or not I would want to live in Chicago, I told him that the only way I would move away with another man is if I was married to him." Morgan smiled, holding her connected hands up to her chest. "And that is when he pulled it out...the ring. He pulled it out of his pocket and said to me, *That's exactly what I hoped you would say.* Girl, it was so romantic. He already knew I was gon' say yes. You should

23

have seen the look on his face. Girl, it was even snowing outside when he did it with the wind blowin' and stuff. It really was like something out of a movie…like a dream come true or something."

Shawna looked away, shaking her head. "Well," she said, trying to process all of that. On one hand, she was happy that her sister had found a guy that she was really into, and a guy who appeared to be somewhat good. However, the last thing in the world that she ever thought would happen would be her walking through the front door after going out to breakfast with him and saying that she was getting married. "Congratulations, I guess," Shawna said, forcing a smile. "It just seems too quick. I mean…it is so quick."

Morgan could pick up on her sister's vibes. And it was obvious that she indeed was trying to be happy for her. Morgan had known, though, that Shawna was probably not going to take this news in the best way. She did not understand, judging by the look on her face, just how deeply Morgan and Chris were in love with one another. They were practically soulmates that God had run across one another in the least likely ways. However, at the same time, the demise of Shawna's relationship with Tron – well, it actually went down in flames – would surely be something that would taint Shawna's perception of it all. Morgan knew, though, to just let her have some time. She gripped her sister's knee.

"Shawna," Morgan said, in a loving way. "You know you gon' be my maid of honor."

Shawna looked at Morgan and smiled. She hugged her sister, knowing that it was the right thing to do. "Awe," she said. "Thank you so much. But, Morgan, I…. I… I just don't know if you have thought this through all that much. I mean, it is only the middle of February. You two have only been serious for like six weeks, or so. Am I right? How can you be sure that you want to marry this guy?" Shawna stood up and headed into the kitchen to put her now-empty glass into the sink. By the time she turned around, Morgan was up and standing in the kitchen doorway.

"What you mean, Shawna?" Morgan asked. "I'm not gonna let the good one get away so I can be embarrassed by the no-good one."

Instantly, Shawna could feel a little tension in the way her sister said that. It was clear that she was insinuating something. And whatever she was insinuating was something that was directed at Shawna.

"What are you try'na say, Morgan?" Shawna asked.

"I'm not try'na say nothing," Morgan said. "All I'm saying is that I'm not gonna let the good guy go when I can go with him. I'm not gonna wait until the no-good guy wastes like three or more years of my life then look around and wonder where all of the good black guys are."

"Hold up," Shawna said. "You talkin' to me like that is what I did on purpose or something. Now, all of the sudden, you want to act like you always thought that Tron was no good or something...like you was always try'na warn me about him or something."

Morgan shook her head, not liking to see her older sister take what she was saying personal. "That's not what I really meant, Shawna," Morgan said. "All I'm sayin' is that I want you to invest your time and energy into getting with a good guy. I mean, girl, look at you. There are niggas downtown, working in them office buildings, who would gladly wife up a black chick like you. And there you are you foolin' around with a nigga who used to deal drugs, and now him and his buddy done used that money to get into the hoe business by owning strip clubs and shit. I know, it's legal and all... I'm not sayin' that it ain't. But, at the same time, you got to know that bein' with somebody like that is gonna come with some problems. You don't really think that THOT Desirae or whatever was the only chick that he was fuckin, do you? The chick that done stabbed the nigga with a fork and made the damn news for it?"

Shawna shook her head and looked down at the floor. "No," she said, hesitantly. "At this point, not really. And I'm passed all that at this point. I'm not gon' be that chick who tries to stand in the way of a man who is try'na start a family and stuff. I admit it...I thought about it for a split second. I was just goin' through the emotions – you know, not thinking straight, is all." Shawna waved her hands. "I'm just sayin' that since I been through a little more than you, I was just try'na help. I'm just keepin' it real with you. It do seem like six weeks is a little too damn soon to be getting married, no matter how old you are or how much the two of you connect with one another and shit. Have you told Mama yet? Have you told Mama that this Chris guy done proposed to you?"

"Well, actually," Morgan said. "I was gon' wait to tell her that, if you wanna know the truth, Shawna. I was gon' wait."

"Wait?" Shawna asked, wanting to know what she meant. "You was going to wait to tell Mama when? Huh? When was you thinkin' that you was gon' tell her that your boo thang has put a ring on it? And it all went down in six weeks. You know Mama is gon... Mama is gon jump on you, probably. Girl, I hope you prepared for it. I swear to God, I hope you are."

"Girl, ain't nobody scared of mama," Morgan said, rolling her eyes. "I swear, you be doin' the most."

"So, when?" Shawna asked. "When was you gon' tell Mama, then? Huh, Morgan?"

Morgan looked away. "Well," she said, hesitantly. "I was thinkin' of tellin' her on the wedding day. You see, Chris has to start this job by the first of April, or sometime around then, I think."

Shawna looked at her sister in disbelief. "So," she said. "You actually try'na get married in six weeks, to a man that you really only been serious with for six weeks? Is that what is goin' on?"

"Shawna," Morgan said, hyperventilating. "Ain't no need to go puttin' all them numbers on it. Love is love, and that is all it is. There ain't no reason I can't go with him, is there? No. Exactly."

Shawna snickered – a snicker that soon turned into a full blown laugh. "Girl, you are crazy," Shawna said, as she pushed passed her sister and went back to chilling on the couch in the living room. "You is a fool, girl. I swear to God, you are. We gon' have to see how this goes."

26

Morgan came back into the room and sat back down on the couch where she had been sitting minutes earlier. "Oh, Shawna," Morgan said. "I knew you was gon' be actin' this way. This is your first Valentine's Day without Tron. You over there going through withdrawals, ain't you?"

Shawna looked at her sister. Her facial expression let her know right then that whatever Morgan had just said was pure foolishness. "Girl, boo," Shawna said. "I'm good. I'm over it."

Morgan squinted at her sister, knowing that she was putting on a front. "Hmm, hmm," she said. "Okay, then. If you say so."

"I am," Shawna said. "I told you about what happened at the club. I feel embarrassed all over again. Then the bitch is havin' his baby, and she crazy as fuck too. I mean, what kinda chick stabs a nigga with a fork?"

"A side chick!" Morgan answered. "You know the bitch already was unstable or fucked up in the head. You saw the way she was actin', and walkin', that day we went up to Clarke's. Plus, she attacked you while she was at work, so now she pregnant and ain't got no job. The bitch is just dumb. I swear to God she dumb as fuck."

"Yeah," Shawna said, thinking about her various interactions with Tron's side chick, Desirae. While the chick was definitely not the kind of woman that Shawna would want to be friends with, Shawna did kind of start to feel sorry for her. Not only had Tron betrayed Shawna, but he had also strung along and made a fool of another young black woman. And, for that reason, Shawna could feel a little bit of what she was going through. "I'm with'chu when you right," Shawna said to her sister. "So, why did you come back from breakfast so early? I mean, damn."

"Cause," Morgan said, liking that the mood had now changed. "Like I told you, he had to go into work. Apparently, he had arranged to have the first half of the day off so that we could go to breakfast together on actual Valentine's Day. I'mma see him, later on when he gets done with his mama."

27

"His mama?" Shawna asked, putting Desirae out of her mind. "What in the world is he doin' with his mama on Valentine's Day?"

"Oh, nothin' crazy," Morgan answered. "He take his mama out to eat on Valentine's Day if she ain't busy or whatever. Tonight, they goin' to some restaurant – soul food, I think – that she like. Then, after that, we gon' meet up and chill for a little bit."

"Yeah," Shawna said. "Guess y'all gotta start planning for the wedding and stuff."

Just then, Morgan's phone began to ring. She rolled her eyes and told Shawna to cut it out right before she picked the phone up and answered. It was her friend, Janae. Within a matter of seconds, Morgan was up and pacing around in her bedroom as she told the entire breakfast engagement story over again as if it was her first time telling it. Shawna now sat on the couch, alone on Valentine's Day for the first time. After glancing at her phone and realizing that she would soon be heading to the shop to do Ms. Susan's hair, she thought about how she truly wished that she could be happy for Morgan. Deep down, she was indeed happy. However, she could not help but to secretly wish that she and Tron's relationship had continued on that course. In fact, that course was the very way she thought that their relationship was headed. Shawna simply gazed out of the living room window, at the snowy February weather, until she got up to get ready to go make a little money.

***

To Shawna's surprise, Ms. Susan was actually waiting out in her car when she pulled into the parking lot of the hair salon. Usually, Shawna had to wait for Ms. Susan, cutting her a little slack and not charging her a late fee because she kept her hair on point – a habit that made Shawna quite a bit of money at times. She did think it was strange that Ms. Susan was available to have her hair done on Valentine's Day since she was seeing a man over in Ohio, in Dayton. However, Shawna then remembered that Ms. Susan was simply living the older version of Desirae's life. Ms. Susan was seeing a man that did not really belong to her, either. While Shawna sort of struggled to really understand why a woman of Ms. Susan's class and caliber would stoop to doing such a thing, she also looked at it from a different point of view: she could learn about the mentality of a woman who is okay with being a side chick.

Shawna walked up to Susan's car and got her attention. Within seconds, Susan was turning her car engine off and climbing out.

"Damn, girl," Susan said. "I didn't see you pull into the parking lot." Susan walked up and gave Shawna a quick hug before the two of the walked side by side to the door of the building. "Girl, I was gon' wait inside. But when I saw that what's her name was the only one in there, I thought I would just sit out in the car and wait. Fuck that bitch, excuse my language."

Shawna chuckled under her breath and lightly shook her head. She looked at Ms. Susan. "Miss Susan," she said. "Wait till I tell you this. Just wait, girl. Just wait."

Ms. Susan could hardly contain herself, wanting to hear whatever details Shawna had for her. Since the night when Tron had been stabbed with a fork at the club, Shawna had not seen Ms. Susan. Once her own feelings calmed down from it, she knew that she would have to tell Ms. Susan. Soon enough, once Shawna got into doing Susan's hair and the other stylist in the shop was leaving, Shawna spilled all of the details...fork and all.

"You are fuckin' kiddin' me," Susan said, not believing the story. "Shawna, girl, is you lying or tellin' the truth. Please tell me that you lyin'... that you makin' this shit up."

"I swear to God, Miss Susan," Shawna said. "If I was not there, I would not believe it either. I watched it all go down, with my own eyes. That bitch got arrested and everything. Her own best friend was there, trying to get with Tron, too, I guess."

Susan shook her head. "That don't make no damn sense," she said. "But I know how, whatever her name is, feels... the THOT."

Shawna giggled. "Miss Susan," she said. "What I tell you about using these words you hear on the radio and stuff, girl?"

Susan laughed. "I got ears," she said. "I hear what is goin' on. So, it sound like to me, that the nigga done gone and got himself a trap queen."

Shawna lightly tapped Ms. Susan's shoulder. "Stop," she said, playfully. "But, yeah, basically. He done got trapped already. It sound like they made it official and stuff when I got there. I'm so done with it. I swear to God, I am."

"And you said that her best friend was there, too?" Susan asked.

Shawna nodded her head, making eye contact with her in the mirror as she worked on the back of her head. "Yep."

Susan shook her head. "That kinda shit don't make no fuckin' sense," she said. "Excuse my language. But it is a shame how a woman always got to worry about her best friend trying to get with her man. I don't know what the hell is up with that shit...excuse me."

"Well, Miss Susan," Shawna said. "I was thinkin' bout you and why you was try'na get your hair done on Valentine's Day. You my only client that was try'na get her hair done on Valentine's Day. All my other clients came swoopin' in last week and over the weekend so they could be flawless for today. What is your story, girl?"

Susan shrugged. "Well," she said hesitantly.

Already, Shawna could tell that Ms. Susan was trying to come up with what she was going to say. "Miss Susan?" Shawna asked, again, after hearing the hesitation. "So, what is your story?"

"You know my story, girl," Susan said. "And I don't need you makin' me feel guilty about it. I just don't, Shawna."

"I ain't try'na make you feel guilty, Miss Susan," Shawna said, hating that her favorite client would say something like that, let alone actually think it. "Why you say that?"

"Because," Susan said. "I sit here and listen to you and all your *Young and the Restless* stuff you have going on. And I think that I'm supposed to be the role model, but I just don't feel like I am. I am old enough to be your mother and here I am, tellin' you about how I'm talking to some dude in Ohio who is already taken...who don't belong to me, no way."

"So," Shawna said, deciding this was her chance to go in for the kill and find out the motivation behind that kind of stuff. "Why do you do that? I'm not judging; I just want to understand. While part of me is really pissed at Tron's side chick, more-so because he kept it from me and carried on with it for however long, I can't help but to feel...to feel...to feel sorry for her. When I see her and what all of this is doing to her, I kinda feel sorry for it. And, don't take this the wrong way, but that makes me kinda think about you. You know that you deserve better than being some woman on the side for a man, Miss Susan. Why do you do it? Why do you go along with that and let these niggas – excuse me, *men* is the word I should use – think that doin' that sorta thing is just okay?"

Susan looked down at the floor, wishing she had an answer already prepared. However, she did not. She knew, at this point, that honesty would truly have to be the best policy.

"Well," Susan said, hesitantly. "Sometimes I want to get married again, and sometimes I don't. Most of the time, if you want the truth, I don't. I mean, it sounds fun, especially since I don't have small children and stuff, but actually getting it to happen is harder than it seems. You will see as you get older. The older you get, the harder it is to meet somebody. And that is really true for this redneck-ass city. There just ain't as many men to choose from like what I would have back in Baltimore with everything that is going on out there and it being close to Washington D.C. I done had a couple white men try to holler. Hey now! But you know how that goes. I just don't know if I can get in bed and marry one of them. I just don't know."

"So, you just like it because it is no pressure on your end?" Shawna asked, wanting clarification. "Is that what I'm hearing?"

"Basically," Susan said, nodding her head. "I mean, if he lived here in the city, I might not be involved like that, but he don't. He live an hour away, in a whole 'nother state, and has a whole 'nother life going on there. I don't have to know what is going on and what he is doing, and who he is doing it with. All I have to do is be available when he got a little time to spend with me. Plus, you know, Miss Susan gets tired of being alone, too, right? I get tired of that, too. And, from the sounds of it, it don't sound like his wife is keeping him all that happy, if you want the truth."

The last part of what Ms. Susan said hit a bit of a sore spot with Shawna. Sure, she did her best at hiding it so that Susan would not pick up on how she was feeling. However, with hearing that his wife must not be keeping him happy, Shawna could not help but think about how Desirae must have been thinking the very same thing when it came to Tron. When the two of them had talked, and gone over to jump on him to really give it to him, Shawna definitely saw that was the impression that Desirae had been under. It hurt a little because she really thought that she was doing everything she could to keep Tron happy. Shawna had even thought she was open enough for communication so that if he was not happy with something, he would feel comfortable talking to her about it so that they could work on it rather than him going out and keeping a chick on the side.

"I see," Shawna said, in a cumbersome tone. "Well, if you happy with that, then so am I, I guess."

"I'm just happy I ain't got to be alone all the damn time like I was for so long," Susan confessed. "It gets hard after a while, you know? But, I will tell you this, that this sister is keeping her eye open for when Mister Right comes along. I'm just playing with this nigga for right now, but I'm not going to be like some of these other women who try to keep a man that did not belong to her in the first place. I promise you, the very second the right brother comes along, Miss Susan is going to snatch him up without a second thought and drop the nigga in Dayton like a bad habit."

Shawna snickered, loving each and every time she got to enjoy Ms. Susan's company.

"Oh," Shawna said. "That reminds me. I got more I gotta tell you."

"More?" Susan asked. "Girl, y'all young people nowadays, with the Facebook and the Instagram and the THOT business really do stay busy, don't you? What is it

32

now? I swear, y'all could have your own reality show. You know what they say, right? Pain pays nowadays."

"No, Miss Susan," Shawna said. "No reality show for me. But, anyway, like I was saying, you are not gon' believe who is getting married after only knowing the guy for six weeks…and is going to pull the wedding off by the first of April. Just guess?"

"Who?" Susan asked, wanting to know.

"My sister, Morgan," Shawna said. "Her boo thang proposed to her this morning when the two of them went out for a Valentine's Day breakfast."

"Aw hell naw," Susan said, not realizing that she had moved her head. Soon enough, she felt the heat of the hot comb touch her scalp for a split second. She winced at the painful feeling before she continued on. "Girl, you a lie," she said. "Morgan try'na marry some nigga that she done only known for like six weeks?"

Shawna nodded. "Hmm, hmm," she answered. "I told her that she is crazy."

"Well," Susan said, smirking. "Sound like the nigga musta had some good dick."

Shawna was shocked to hear such language come out of Ms. Susan's mouth. She stopped for a second to playfully slap Ms. Susan's shoulder. "Miss Susan," Shawna said. "Your language, girl. I can't believe I just heard you say something like that. Oh my God."

"Girl, whatever," Ms. Susan said. "I only said it cause I know that is exactly what you was thinking. Why else would you marry a man that you have only known for six weeks? For all she know, he could have some kids or a secret wife and family or some stuff in Oklahoma or somewhere. Girl, you betta tell her that I said that she better do her research before she walk down that aisle. I don't know about nobody marrying somebody after six weeks."

"She says she loves him, Miss Susan," Shawna told her. "And that he got some job in Chicago that he was not gon' take unless his boo thang go with him, you know?"

"A betta job?" Ms. Susan asked. "In Chicago? Well, Shawna, damn. That changes everything. You ain't say all that. He might just be makin' some real money, then. If that's the case, she betta go on and jump on that train until she with him at the bank and putting her name on the dotted line so that she can have access to the money and stuff. You said they try'na get married in six weeks?"

"Yep," Shawna said. "He gotta take the job by April first, so they try'na get this done and over with quick."

"Six weeks is long enough to get to know somebody," Susan said. "She'll be alright."

Shawna shook her head, knowing that Ms. Susan was only seeing the dollar signs of Morgan's crazy situation.

"So, Tron is still on your mind, huh?" Susan asked. "I can tell that he is."

Shawna shook her head. "Naw," she answered. "He ain't."

"Girl, stop frontin'," Susan told Shawna. "If he wasn't, you would not have asked me about me and mine. I ain't stupid, girl. I know, I know. You ain't got to lie to me."

"Well," Shawna said. "It's not that he is on my mind, but, you know, it's Valentine's Day."

"And you feelin' all sappy and shit?" Susan asked. "Excuse my language, girl."

"Sort of," Shawna admitted. "It's my first time being alone on Valentine's Day in a long time."

"Do you still love Tron, Shawna?" Susan came right on out and asked. "Tell me the truth. Don't think about what all has happened and how you think you supposed to feel based on what society tells you that you should feel. Look deep in your heart. I know you're hurt and all that – been there, done that. But, tell me this, and be honest with yourself: Do you still love him?"

Shawna stopped what she was doing and looked up, into the mirror. She and Susan's eyes met as Shawna took a moment to think. "Maybe," she said, as she looked back down into Ms. Susan's hair. "But I can't get back with him. Not after what he did. I would never look at him the same way again. Never."

Chapter 3

Tron forgot how much he enjoyed spending time with his daughter Ebony. Ever since he and Andria had broken up, things had been kind of dicey. Sure, the two of them were somewhat co-parenting well at this point. However, it took quite a bit of cursing, and a few public scenes, for either of them to get to this point. On Friday, Andria had driven Ebony up from Louisville so that the little girl could spend the weekend with her father. It really was not the best time for Tron to spend time with his daughter, with being stabbed at the club a little less than two weeks ago. However, he knew that he could really smooth her over for a while if he made her birthday present on Valentine's Day.

Tron looked in his rearview mirror at Ebony. The little brown-skinned girl, with a missing tooth in her smile, looked up at her father when she heard him speak. "So, what did you decide?" Tron asked. "You want pizza or Applebee's." He remembered exactly what kind of food his daughter liked, trying to make sure that she got it each day that she was staying with him.

"I don't know, Daddy," Ebony said.

"Well, you need to decide," Tron told her. "Daddy is coming up on the highway and he is either gonna go left or right, so you better hurry up."

"Applebee's!" Ebony announced, as if it were going out of style. "Let's go to Applebee's. I wanna go there, Daddy."

Tron chuckled and looked back at the road ahead of him. "Okay," he said, smiling. "No problem."

On the highway, Tron made sure to continue conversation with his daughter. Even if he couldn't really think of anything to talk about, he would make her think of something. As he drove up Interstate 64, toward the northwest side of the city, all he could think about was how fast his daughter was growing up. And he could not even say that she was growing up before his eyes. He did not get to see her all that often, or at least as often as he would like. And, at this point in his life, he sometimes regretted some of his choices that led to that. Tron did not like the idea of being one of those men who had children in different cities and states. Something about that just had never appealed to him. Now, with Desirae's crazy ass pregnant, that is exactly what Tron would be.

Since getting out of the hospital and declining to press charges against Desirae for stabbing him at the club, Tron now felt as if he had a chip on his shoulder. At certain points, as he and his daughter headed to Applebee's, he found it incredibly difficult to focus on what she was saying. Something – be it a word or the name of a street or the information on a billboard – would always trip him up mentally and make him think about Desirae. And his thoughts were not flattering, to say the least.

Because of Desirae, his club had been royally embarrassed. Tron practically kicked himself every day for not figuring out that something was unstable about that girl. He hated that he had not picked up on all of the signs before he got in deep with her, keeping her on the side as a permanent thing to do. Now, more than ever, Tron was sure that she had purposely gotten pregnant by him. Desirae may never admit it, but at least that's what he thought. In fact, he had no problem believing that is exactly what she did. He had actually had a peaceful couple of weeks without talking to her – a couple of weeks that he would probably not say was worth being stabbed with a fork for, though. However, Tron knew that the silence would eventually have to come to an end. That woman – whoever she is, was, or will be – is pregnant by him. Every so often, Tron would try to think up ways that he could bring up a paternity test. He was still at a loss, but knew that he had time to think about it some more.

"Daddy, you hear me?" Ebony broke through her father's train of thought saying, "When are you gonna take me on the trip?"

Fuck, Tron thought. He remembered promising to take Ebony on a trip, but did not think that she would actually remember and hold him to it. As he thought about it for a second, trying to come up with an answer, the idea crossed his mind that Andria was probably keeping that hope alive in Ebony. She could be a sneaky little bitch. There was no doubt about that.

"Soon, Ebony," Tron said. "Soon. When Daddy got time away from his businesses and stuff, and the weather is not so cold and icy and snowy, Daddy is gonna swoop down and pick his little girl up. Have you thought about where you wanna go? Somewhere warm, right." Somewhere warm, Tron actually hoped.

"No," Ebony said. "I read about some islands, but I still don't know where I wanna go to yet. I will think about it and let you know."

"Some islands?" Tron said, sounding surprised. "How are we going to get to islands if cars can't drive across water?"

"Planes, Daddy," Ebony responded. "We can take a plane. It's easy."

"Easy, huh?" Tron said, his voice lowering. Right then, he knew that Andria was planting stuff in Ebony's head then watering it so it would grow.

"Daddy?" Ebony started. "Where is Shawna? Did she go out of town or something? When am I going to see Shawna?"

Fuck, Tron thought. *This was the very topic I have been trying to steer her away from for the last three days.*

Tron had actually thought the entire weekend would pass without Ebony bringing Shawna back up. She had asked about Shawna when Andria first dropped her off – maybe another one of Andria's seeds. However, just as she was asking, Tron took the opportunity of carrying her stuff upstairs then coming back down to talk to Andria about some parental stuff to make her forget about it. Since then, Tron had kept her busy enough to where by the time she got home, she went right to sleep in his bed.

"Yeah, sort of," Tron lied, knowing how much his little girl Ebony loved Shawna.

"Oh, okay," Ebony said. "So, when is she coming back? Will she be back before I go back home?"

Tron cringed under his breath. "I don't know," he answered. "I don't know. I don't know when she's coming back. And she had already planned to leave on her trip before me and your mama planned for you to come up here. I talked to her though…" Tron took a moment to think about where he could take this. "And she said that she hopes she comes back before you leave."

"Good," Ebony said, liking what she heard. "I hope she comes back soon."

Within ten minutes or so, Tron was pulling into the parking lot of Applebee's. Since it was in the middle of the day, on a weekday, the restaurant was not crowded, which Tron liked. Quickly, he helped Ebony out of the car and they went inside, a hostess seating the two of them in a booth on the side. As soon as Tron had ordered drinks for the two of them, he could feel his phone vibrating in his pocket.

"So, how is your mom's side of the family?" Tron asked, trying to keep Ebony busy as she colored on the complementary coloring sheet.

As Ebony began to talk about her grandparents and aunts and uncles, Tron pulled his phone out of his pocket. He tried to get to it before it stopped vibrating. Just as he was about to unlock the screen to answer, he saw who was calling him: Desirae.

Tron glanced up at Ebony and nodded before looking back down into his phone screen. Without seconds, the MISSED CALL alert popped up. Behind it was an UNREAD MESSAGE icon. Tron unlocked his phone and went straight to the text messages. It, just like the call he had just ignored, was Desirae. The text message read: *Enough of this cold war shit, nigga. We need to talk. ASAP.*

Tron shook his head, deciding to just put his phone back into his pocket. He was going to enjoy his time with his daughter. Desirae would just have to wait. Furthermore, Tron believed that Desirae should be grateful that a nigga did not decide to press charges. He knew that he took the higher road with that situation – decided to be the more mature one.

"Well, that's good," Tron said, after picking up on Ebony saying that her Uncle Pete was opening another restaurant in Lexington. "Make sure you tell them that Daddy said hello."

"I will," Ebony said.

Ebony went on talking about some friends on her street in Louisville, names that Tron had only heard in passing. Yet again, Tron felt his phone vibrating. He pulled his phone out of his pocket and saw that it was Desirae calling again.

"Damn," Tron said, almost whispering to himself. He knew that if Desirae was calling back to back after all of this time, she was in one of her bratty moods. Desirae was the kind of chick that would call ten times if she had to, just to be noticed.

Tron pressed IGNORE. Then, just like the first time, Tron saw that he had an UNREAD MESSAGE text alert. He unlocked his phone and went to MESSAGES. Once again, it was a text from Desirae – a new message. This one read: *We need to talk, ASAP. Went to the doctor today.*

Tron positioned his hands on his phone to begin to text Desirae. He paused for a moment as he thought of what he wanted to say. He did not like the idea of the mother of his child going to the doctor on her own, as if the father was not present. However, much of that was Desirae's fault. After a few seconds, Tron decided to just suck it up and text her back: *With my daughter right now. Will text you back later.*

After sending that message, several minutes passed without a message popping up on his phone from Desirae. Eventually, he figured that she, for once, decided to be classy and show respect by not interrupting him if she knew that he was with his daughter. *Praise be*, Tron thought, remembering what his church-going aunt used to say all of the time when he was a kid.

Soon enough, Tron and Ebony had placed their order with the waitress. As the waitress, who was a thick and shapely white girl with an okay face, walked away, Tron checked her out. He had never really been all that into white women. However, as he had problems with black women from time to time, he sometimes wondered what it would be like on the other side, so to speak. From what he had heard, white women knew how to take care of a man. He just didn't know if he could get down with any woman that did not have a black woman's ass, skin tone and all.

While Tron and Ebony waited on their food to come, Ebony stopped talking as much as she did. Tron couldn't help but notice. "Ebony," he said. "Why are you quiet now?"

Ebony shrugged. "You're not listening, anyway," she answered. "So, I'll just stop talking."

"I'm not listening?" Tron asked. "What makes you think that Daddy ain't listening to you?"

"All day we been gone," Ebony said. "It's like you don't do much talking. And now, you keep looking at your phone."

"Ebony," Tron said. "You know Daddy gotta check his phone. It might be about money. You know that."

"I know, I know," Ebony said. "That's why I didn't say anything. Are you okay, though?"

The skin on Tron's forehead wrinkled. He wanted to understand why his daughter would be asking him if he was okay. At her age, she ought not to know the difference, or so Tron thought.

"What do you mean am I okay?" Tron asked.

"Just cause," Ebony said. "I don't know. Just seems like you're not okay."

Tron had already decided that he was not going to tell Andria or Ebony about being stabbed at the club. It was already on the local news. Tron could only pray that it hadn't been a slow news day that day down in Louisville. There wasn't much reason for the news down there to cover it otherwise. It had been nearly two weeks at this point and he had not heard anything out of his family or friends that he still kept in touch with in Louisville. He was cool with that.

"I mean," Tron said, looking at his little girl and realizing that she was really growing up. "Daddy's just got a lot of stress right now. But I don't want you to worry about it. It's nothing serious, okay?"

"Okay," Ebony said.

Tron played around with his Ebony, trying to see if she could name all fifty states. She named just about all of the states in the Midwest area, probably because she heard the most about them. Then she named places like California and New York and Florida and Hawaii – popular places that were far away. Tron helped her through words like Massachusetts and Connecticut. She still struggled with Mississippi, no matter how hard she tried. Time flew by until their food arrived.

As Tron and Ebony were eating, Ebony began to ramble a bit. Tron zoned back in when she began to talk about her mother.

"Yeah, so we might be moving to there in the spring," Ebony said.

"To where?" Tron asked, wanting to quickly catch up.

"In with mommy's boyfriend," Ebony said.

Tron stopped for a minute, wondering why he did not know that Andria was getting serious with another man. Even if he could not be in his daughter's life on a daily basis, he still did not like the idea of her mother living with a man that he did not know.

"Oh, yeah?" Tron asked. "What's Mommy's boyfriend's name? Daddy forgets, so you have to remind me."

"Eric, Daddy," Ebony said. "Everybody knows that."

"Oh, does everybody?" Tron asked, rhetorically. "Isn't that interesting." Just then, Tron thought back to when Andria had dropped Ebony off on Friday. He had specifically asked her if there was anything that he should know. And of all the thing she brought up, going on and on about things that were really irrelevant, Tron found it interesting how she did not bring up the idea of her and Ebony moving in with another man. "So," Tron started, wanting to know more. "How long has Mommy been dating Eric?"

Ebony shrugged as she ate her food. "I don't know," she answered. "I met him some months ago now, back when it was around Halloween."

"Oh," Tron said. "Okay."

Tron slid his phone out of his pocket, feeling a little aggravated that Andria did not mention this. He sent a text message to her: *When are you moving in with Eric?* Tron dropped his phone back into his pocket, deciding that he would simply check for her reply later on.

"Well," Tron said to Ebony. "I'mma have to talk to Mommy about that."

"Why?" Ebony asked. "Why you gotta talk to Mommy about it, Daddy?"

"Cause," Tron said. "Daddy cares about who you live with, so I just need to talk to Mommy about it."

41

"Well, Mommy and me was talking about me coming here," Ebony said. "But I don't know when and stuff."

"Comin' where?" Tron asked, totally confused at what his daughter was saying. "What are you talking about, Ebony? Comin' where?"

"Up here," Ebony told him. "Up to Indianapolis, to live with you. Mommy and me was talking about it for a while, but she hasn't said anything for a long time now."

"Oh, she hasn't?" Tron said. "I'mma have to talk to Mommy about some of this."

Tron thought long and hard for a few moments about any possible way that his little girl would misunderstand something like moving up to Indianapolis. What could she have confused it with? Could she have misheard? These were all questions that Tron wanted answers to. His life was not set up in any way for him to be taking on the responsibility of taking care of his daughter. Before he would ever think of doing something like that, he would have to make sure that Desirae is straight. And doing this was something that he already knew was not going to be easy. His boy Tyrese had clowned him when he got out of the hospital, telling him that he was the first nigga in Indianapolis to have made the news for being stabbed by his side chick.

***

Tron pulled up outside of his townhouse. He and Ebony had had a nice little day together. After they finished with lunch at Applebee's, Tron took her over to a friend's house – a friend who had children in the same age group. It was somewhat refreshing for Tron to hang around other adults who were not in the same life as his. While Ebony played with his friend Miles' two kids, the two talked about this and that. Sure, Miles knew that Tron had gone into business with Tyrese to open Honeys East. However, Miles had been a tied-down man for all of his adult life, having gotten married to his high school sweetheart a year after graduation. Tron saw Miles as just a cool dude, and the pair like to go out for drinks every so often.

"I don't see Shawna's car," Ebony said. "She must not be back yet, is she?"

Tron silently cringed as he turned the car off. Every time his little girl said something about Shawna, a glint of guilt would zip through his body. Then and only then, he would begin to feel a little anger. In his eyes, Desirae was the one who messed up this entire situation. And Desirae would be the one that Tron would have to deal with for the next two decades. Tron was sure that she had been texting or calling him as he felt his phone vibrate in his pocket while he drove home.

"Naw, Ebony," Tron said. "She probably ain't comin' back tonight. You know Shawna don't like the snow. And I think it is supposed to snow again tonight, so she gon' prolly get on the road in a couple of days and come back, when it ain't supposed to be snowing like this."

"But I leave tomorrow," Ebony said. "I hope she can come back tomorrow."

"Yeah," Tron said, pushing his car door open. "I do, too," he added. "I do, too. Come on, Ebony. Let's get inside."

Ebony did just as her father said, pushing her own car door open and jumping out onto the crunchy parking lot. She giggled a little when she stepped up onto the sidewalk. Tron noticed and got an idea. Quickly, he bent over, grabbed a handful of snow and patted it softly until it was shaped like a ball. Gently, he tossed the snowball at his daughter. She laughed as the ball collided with her coat before falling to the ground.

"Daddy!" Ebony yelled, smiling. "Why you do that? You ain't seen my snowballs, have you?"

"What snowballs?" Tron asked, acting surprised. "You can't make no damn snowballs... Not like me, you can't."

"Oh yeah?" Ebony said, ready to show her daddy that he was dead wrong. "Watch this!"

Just then, Ebony kneeled down into the snow and began to make her own snowball. Tron watched, smiling, wishing that he could have these kinds of experiences with his daughter every day. As she made the snowball, she pumped herself up, talking about just how good it was going to be. Within a matter of seconds, Ebony actually had a pretty decent snowball put together, to where Tron was nodding his

43

head and recognizing that his baby girl had indeed inherited some things from her father. He could not help but smile.

"Okay, okay," Tron said, nodding.

Just as Tron looked away, a car turning into the parking lot of his apartment community got his attention, he felt Ebony's snowball come right toward his face. He ducked, causing the snowball to hit him on the side of his head. He quivered a little from feeling the little chunks of snow get into his ear. All the while Tron got back on his game from being clobbered with Ebony's snowball, Ebony laughed, jumping up and down where she stood.

When Tron looked back at his daughter, having fully recuperated from the surprise attack, he nodded and gave her props. Just as he was bending down to make another snowball, he noticed a car pull into a parking spot across from where he and his daughter played together. Immediately, he recognized it as a car that he knew. In fact, it was the same car that he had noticed turning the corner when Ebony hit him with her snowball in the first place.

"Desirae," Tron said, totally zoned out from whatever Ebony was saying.

There could never have been a worse time than right now for Desirae to roll up and park outside of Tron's place. He was sure there was no way she could have found out that his daughter would be in town this particular weekend, on this particular day, which was Monday. Tron almost wanted to look up at the sky and say "God, why me?" However, his eyes were locked on the rear of Desirae's car. He knew that in a matter of seconds, she would be climbing out of the front seat and forcing herself into a situation. She had become rather good at forcing herself into situations where she had no place being, and her doing so left this bitter taste in Tron's mouth.

Just then, Tron felt another snowball hit him. He put on a smile and looked at Ebony, seeing that she was still in the happiest mood that he had probably seen her in many years. Just as Tron was coming up with something to say about getting her inside, he could hear a car door open – Desirae's car door. Immediately, the sound of crunching feet came closer. Tron's nostrils flared as he thought to himself about

44

how hard it was about to be for him to not lose his cool with her.

"Ebony, we better get you inside so you don't get sick," Tron said. However, it was now too late. Desirae was practically about to step onto the sidewalk, her presence having grabbed Ebony's attention.

Desirae walked up to Tron. She smiled, looking at a father and daughter interact with one another in a Hallmark-movie way. It was sweet. She rubbed her hands together and looked at Tron.

"Hey, Tron," Desirae said. She then leaned in, forcing Tron to hug her briefly so things would not look strange to his daughter.

"Wassup?" Tron said, clearly not even wanting to hear anything that Desirae had to say. If he did not answer the phone, nor any of her text messages, then why would she think that it would be okay to just show up at his place? This chick was really testing his patience.

"Oh, just out and about today, Tron," Desirae said. "And I was calling you, but I didn't know if your phone was off or something. So, I was just riding through the area and thought that I'll just stop and see if you were home. If you were, then great. If not, I'd just catch up with you later." She opened her arms, pointing toward Ebony and Tron. "And look what I rolled up on. You out here, playing with your niece."

Tron looked at Desirae, wishing that he had never been led down a path of even knowing her. At this point, the very thing that attracted him to her in the first place – her body – was something that he could not even appreciate anymore, or at least not in the same way that he used to. Her demeanor had changed so much that she was now just unpleasant. Furthermore, purposely trapping him really put her onto his "bad" list. He specifically remembered telling her that he had a daughter who lived down south. Why would she walk up saying anything about a niece? Tron could see what Desirae was really trying to do. No sooner than he could look at Ebony, she was already saying something.

"I'm not his niece," Ebony said, smiling. "I'm his daughter."

"Oh," Desirae said. She smiled, with her eyes open wide, trying to be as nice as possible while she talked to the little girl. "Well, excuse me. I don't think we've ever met, have we? I thought he had a niece about your age. And what did you say that your name was?"

"Ebony," she answered, proudly.

Desirae reached out and shook the little girl's hand. "Okay, then," she said. "Ain't you so cute. I'm Desirae." She glanced up at Tron. "I'm a special friend of your father," she added, just as she stood back up.

"Yeah," Tron said, now visibly angry. "Ebony, let me let you on inside so you won't be gettin' sick before you go back home to your mother. Definitely don't need that problem."

Not even looking into Desirae's eyes, Tron pulled his keys out of his pocket and signaled to Ebony that she needed to follow him. Ebony waved goodbye to Desirae, with Desirae waving back, as she followed her father up and inside of the house. After Tron told Ebony to make a sandwich while he talked to his friend, he turned the heat up a little for her then headed back outside. Now, even though he was out in the bright daylight, he was at least not going to be seen saying anything wrong and disrespectful to another woman with his daughter watching. He prided himself in at least not being that kind of father.

Tron quickly walked up to Desirae, who was still standing on the sidewalk.

"What the fuck do you think you doin'?" Tron asked.

Desirae dropped her pleasant front that she had put up for meeting Ebony. The news she got today trumped whatever little bullshit feelings Tron would call himself feeling. She came here to talk business. It was not her fault that he did not answer the phone when she called, let alone respond to her text messages.

"Tron," Desirae said, shaking her head. "I ain't even come here for no bullshit. But, damn, can you invite a bitch in or something? Why we gotta stand out in the cold talking? Why Tron?"

Tron looked back at his front door then back to Desirae. After getting a quick glance of her shape, he looked back up to her face and shook his head. "I swear you crazy," he said bluntly. "Here I am, spending time with my daughter and shit, and what do you do? Come rollin' up on a nigga, try'na ruin it and shit. What's next? You come to stab me again, Desirae?"

Desirae rolled her eyes. "Damn, nigga," she said. "I told you I was sorry. Get over it. I been callin' you and textin' you to tell you somethin'."

"I know," Tron said. "But why you act like you can't wait till I respond or something. I saw you callin' and shit, but I ain't wanna be rude to my daughter. It's not exactly like we get to spend a lot of time together anyway. This is the longest I done spent with her in a long time. And now I gotta stand out in the snow, talkin' to some bitch who tried to kill me."

Just then, a car rolled by in the parking lot. It was Tron's neighbor across the way, Mr. Trotter, a white man. Quickly, Tron waved and smiled, nodding his head.

"There you go callin' me out my name, Tron," Desirae said. "And you know you just ain't gotta do that. That's what got you in trouble in the first place. Look, I swear I ain't here cause I want no more of that dick or nothin'. It caused more problems than it was worth, if you wanna know the truth. I told you that I went to the doctor today."

"Yeah," Tron said. "I saw the text. And I wanted to know why you ain't tell me that you was goin, but whatever. Prolly just thinkin' about yourself again or some shit. So, what the doctor say?"

Desirae hesitated for a second, looked away and trying to get together just the right amount of energy to tell him what Doctor Adair showed her.

"Well," Desirae said, feeling her confidence come back. "I'm due around late August or early September."

Tron calmed down a little, realizing that being worked up was not going to make anything better at this point. He looked at Desirae' stomach, trying to convince himself that she was pregnant by him and not some other nigga. "Well, that's good," he said, nodding his head. "That's real coo."

"Yeah," Desirae said. "And it's twins."

Twins seemed to be the only word that Tron heard. It echoed in his head as the image of two little babies popped into his mind. He had never known any twins, let alone anyone who raised any. Tron balled his fists, driving them into the sides of his thighs as he turned away.

"What the fuck?" he said, turning back to Desirae. "Twins? Fuckin' twins? Like two babies? Two fuckin' babies?"

Desirae simply remained silent. She nodded her head instead of speaking. She knew that she would need to give Tron a few seconds to process this.

Tron heard Desirae's silence. He could tell by the look on her face, as well as how she was standing and the tone in her voice, that she was indeed telling the truth. He glanced at her stomach, thinking about how there were two babies in there. Tron laughed, shaking his head.

"You gotta be fuckin' shittin' me," Tron said, his lips tight. "This bitch done trapped me and done did it with two babies. Oh my God, you gotta be fuckin' kiddin' me."

"Nigga!" Desirae said, now raising her voice a little bit. "I don't know why you keep sayin' that shit, and I don't know why you been over here thinkin' that stupid ass shit. You know that I ain't trap your ass. I told you. I just forgot that I didn't take my birth control."

"How the fuck you forget something like that?" Tron asked. "How the fuck you forget somethin' like that unless you really just try'na get pregnant by some nigga? Huh? How the fuck you do that?"

Desirae rolled her eyes and shook her head. She found it so pitiful the way that some niggas could act when they find out about their responsibilities. "Well, I don't know," she said, sounding very sarcastic. "Maybe the same way you forgot to put a condom on? I mean, why else would you fuck a chick without a condom unless you was try'na get her pregnant?"

Tron was so mad right now. "I told you the deal when we first startin' fuckin' round, Desirae," he said. "I told your ass that them fuckin' condoms is too tight and that if we was gon' be fuckin' around, that you would have to be on some fuckin' birth control. I even told your ass that I would pay for the shit."

"Look, I'm sorry," Desirae said. "And whatever you think, you just gon' have to deal with. The fact of the matter is that I am pregnant with twins. And I just thought that you should know that I was havin' twins."

"And I still don't even know if they mine or not," Tron said.

Words like that cut right through Desirae. The very idea of a man acting ashamed to have children with her just did not feel good.

"Look, nigga!" Desirae yelled, knowing that she might as well go hard or go home. "I ain't no fuckin' hoe. You was the only nigga that I was fuckin' round with, like I told you. I don't know why you can't believe that. Oh, maybe it is because you was fuckin' round of your chick, Shawna or whatever. So, you think that I had to be doin' the same thing, too, huh? Is that what you think?"

"Man, fuck this shit," Tron said. "Why are you here? Huh? Why you here? Why you couldn't just tell me some shit like this over the phone? I know you want somethin'. Bitches always come back around when they want somethin'. You need some attention, or somethin'?"

"Nigga, fuck you!" Desirae said. In a flash, she started to throw punches at Tron, right there on the sidewalk in front of his townhouse. As any man should, Tron ducked away from Desirae's fists. In the midst of moving away from her, he told her that she was crazy – words that only fueled her rage even more. "I don't need no fuckin' attention from you!" Desirae let him know. "I was comin' over here to tell you that, and to tell you that I would be movin' outta my apartment this weekend and back in with my mama. Thought you might wanna help the future mother of your children so that when I do get back on my feet, I ain't raisin' your kids in no fuckin' project or somewhere far out, in some shitty-ass apartments or somethin'. I'm betta than that, and you know it."

Tron took a few deep breaths and looked up toward the sky. For the last so-many weeks, he indeed had been thinking about what kind of financial moves he would be making. Desirae being pregnant could not have come at a worse time. He was still working on remaking the club – trying to save a sinking ship, so to speak, since the club and its exterior had been in the news lately. On top of that, Shawna moving out on him left him to pay the bills on his own in the dead of winter.

"I know, Desirae," Tron said. "I know. And, like I told you, if the baby, or babies, is mine then I'mma be a man and help you. I'mma make sure that you get whatever you need, whenever you need it. Showin' up at my place, like we fuckin' together or somethin', ain't it, though. I put it on everything, I was going to call you back as soon as my little girl Ebony went to sleep tonight. I ain't wanna take away our time together by being on the phone, or standing outside in the snow, talking to you."

For a moment there, Desirae did start to feel a little childish. If she would have known this his daughter was over to his place, that might of told her that other people could be over too and maybe she would not have come. However, if she was going to be the mother of his children for the next eighteen years, there was no reason she needed to wait when it came to meeting his family. Nothing could be further from the truth than with meeting his daughter.

"Tron," Desirae said. "It is not like I knew you was over here with your daughter. But, I will say this, I do think that she might as well go ahead and meet me and get to know me. After all, she is about to have two siblings because of me. Am I right, or am I wrong?"

"Look, Desirae," Tron said, keeping his voice a little lower and talking in a much smoother tone. "I know you prolly scared and stuff about all of this. And, to tell you the truth, so am I. But if we gon' raise this baby – these babies – together, you gon' have to work with me a little bit."

"Work with you?" Desirae asked, as if she had just heard something crazy come out of Tron's mouth. "You admitted yourself to me just a few minutes ago that you saw that I was callin' you and textin' you and stuff and purposely did not answer. I understand that you were with your daughter, and I respect that. I'm a real woman about my shit, so I really do respect when a man is spending time with his children. But what if I really was needing something, though? And you were just ignoring me like that? You could have just answered and told me what the deal was, you know. We could have arranged some time to meet or whatever, and I swear, I woulda been just fine with all of that. But, no, you already not try'na even work with me by just pushin' me out of your life like you ain't even know me or nothin'."

Tron shook his head. "Girl, you one crazy…I swear," he said, his words full of regret and resentment. "I told you that I was gon' call you when I got home and talk to you. You didn't even tell me that you were goin' to the doctor and stuff. How is that workin' with me, huh? Tell me that. How the fuck is that try'na work with me?"

Desirae hesitated for a moment. She then thought about the couples that she saw out in the waiting room while she sat in anticipation of meeting with Doctor Adair. She then thought about how Tron had really talked a good game to her about them being together, especially since he was basically trapped in an unhappy relationship.

"Look," Desirae said. "We ain't even together, so I don't even know why the fuck you would think that I would have to call you and tell you that I'm goin' to the fuckin' doctor."

"You know what," Tron started, "Whatever." His head shook. "It's whatever. So, you said you movin' out of your apartment this weekend and in with your mama or whatever?"

Desirae nodded. "Yeah," she said. "That's the plan, anyway. Gotta find some help."

"So now you sayin' that you need me to come help you move?" Tron asked.

Desirae shook her head. "Naw," she answered. "That is not what I'm sayin'. I was just lettin' you know."

"I can come help you move if you need me to help you do that, Desirae," Tron said, wishing that he did not feel obligated to help this woman who had basically helped his life, and relationship, just fall to pieces."

"I don't know," Desirae said. "I just don't know. I didn't even know I would be out here talkin' to you today, let alone that you would actually be offerin' to help, especially since we not together."

"And we not gon' be together," Tron let Desirae know. "So, just get that out of your head. We not gon' be together, Desirae."

"Oh, yeah?" Desirae said, snapping her neck back. "Nigga, I don't even know why the fuck you so stuck on thinking that somebody would even want to be with your ass. I'm just over here so that my mind is clear about all of this – so that I know that I gave my kids' father a chance to be a damn daddy to his kids, is all. I swear to God. I don't ever wanna be with you, no fuckin' way. Whatever man I decide to settle down with and dedicate my life to is gonna be the kinda nigga that ain't try'na keep me in no closet, across town, like I'm some secret or something."

"Damn, Desirae," Tron said. He hated how she was so good at playing the victim. "When we first started hookin' up, Desirae, I told your ass what is was and what it was gon' be. You ain't tell me that you was lookin' for some nigga to be with you."

"I know," Desirae said, starting to feel some regret. "I know, I know, I know, Tron. Shit."

Desirae turned away and stepped off of the sidewalk. Within a matter of seconds, Tron was watching Desirae's big ass walk further and further away from him and across the parking lot. Even though he hated the woman's guts and soul with a passion at this very moment, a man was going to be a man. A man would not be able to help himself but to notice Desirae's body of perfection. Even in these two weeks or so since Tron had seen her, he had not seen a chick in the entire city who had a body that could compare. Tron then started to wonder how long it would be before Desirae's body would change – how long before she had gained weight and lost the very thing that she had going for herself.

"I'm outta here," Desirae said, confidently. "I was just stoppin' by anyway, nigga. I ain't mean to hold you up, and you got me standin' outside in the snow like I'm some damn stranger that you can't let come in your ass or no shit. This is whatever." Her head shook. "I'm betta than that."

Tron began to walk toward his door. "Whatever," he said, wanting to hurl curse words at her. "I'll hit you up whenever."

"Yeah, yeah," Desirae said. "Tell little Ebony that your friend said hi."

Tron glanced at Desirae as she climbed into the driver seat of her car. He absolutely hated that she had walked up on him and Ebony and basically introduced herself as if she had every right to be known. "Yeah," Tron said, sounding salty. "I'll do that."

Desirae hopped into her car, pulled out of the parking spot, and disappeared. Tron pushed his front door open, stepped in, and shut it, hard. Once the door was shut and locked, he climbed the stairs. Just as he got halfway up, he could hear his daughter's voice from the living room. She had heard the front door slam shut. Instantly, even though she did not see her father all of the time, the little girl knew that something was definitely wrong. It was strange for her father to shut the door like that. Within a matter of seconds, Ebony had rushed from the living room to the foot of the steps. She now looked up at her father.

"What's wrong, Daddy?" Ebony asked, her eyes practically sparkling in the light that was coming through the windows. "Daddy?"

Tron took a deep breath, knowing that he needed to play it cool with Ebony. He turned around. "Ain't nothin' wrong," Tron said. "Nothin."

"Did your friend, Desirae, leave already?" Ebony asked.

"Yeah," Tron said, finishing his climb to the top of the steps. "Yeah, she gone Ebony. What are you doin' down there?"

"Watchin' the TV," Ebony answered.

"Oh, okay," Tron said. "Well, go on back to watchin' TV and shit. Daddy gotta make some calls and stuff. I'll be down there in a little bit, okay?"

"Okay," Ebony said, smiling. She went back to the living room.

Tron pushed his bedroom door open, stepped inside, and shut it. He covered his face with both of his hands as he shook his head.

"Nigga," he said to himself. "You done really fucked up. That bitch is crazy."

Tron played over the entire interaction with Desirae out on the sidewalk in his head. He sat on the edge of his bed, looking through the blinds of his bedroom window at the snowy outside. No matter where he went – the club, home, or even Desirae's house – he just did not feel like he could relax and get away from a woman with drama. Part of him wanted to snicker, because everything that was going on sounded just that fucking ridiculous. However, another part of him wanted to put one of his fists through a wall. While he would never actually do something like that, he really was just that mad about Desirae getting pregnant by him. What really made it all more worse was that she was pregnant with twins.

"I don't even know if them babies is mine," Tron said.

No matter what Desirae said to Tron, he was still going to find a way to get her to agree to a paternity test. There was just no way that he was going to be one of those niggas you hear about that takes care of a child that they thought was theirs for so many years. At this point in his life, he had so much to lose that doing something like that was definitely the last thing he would ever wish for.

After sitting on the edge of his bed for a few minutes in thought, trying to calm down a little, he knew that he would need a little help with this. He walked over to the door, opened it, and looked downstairs. It did not seem that Ebony would be coming up the stairs anytime soon to bother him. Upon seeing this, Tron pushed the door closed and put a towel along the bottom edge. Soon enough, he was rolling a blunt with some fire weed he had just gotten from his connect on Friday, before Andria had gotten to town and dropped Ebony off.

Tron lit his blunt and looked around his bedroom. There was no denying the elephant in the room: he really did miss Shawna. Something about her not being there really did make his life – his time at home – seem extremely different. He then thought about how he wasn't the only one who hadn't talked to Shawna in the last couple of weeks; Ebony wanted to see her as well. As Tron thought about this, he pulled his phone out of his pocket and began to text Shawna. While he struggled to think of the words to say, he decided that he would simply call her and say what he needed to say. He knew that if he told Shawna that Ebony wanted to see her, she would be nicer than if it was just him asking.

"Hello?" Shawna asked.

"Hey," Tron said, in a soft but deep voice. "It's Tron."

"I know," Shawna said. "I did delete your contact information in my phone, but, of course, I can't delete the phone number from my memory."

"Okay," Tron said, not liking the layer of bitterness he heard in Shawna's voice. "I wasn't callin' to get you back or nothin' like that, so don't start trippin' and thinkin' that. I was actually callin' about somethin' else."

"What?" Shawna asked. She was curious but unenthused. "What is it, Tron?"

"I wanna ask you a favor," Tron said. "Ebony is here."

"Oh," Shawna said. "She is."

"Yeah, Shawna," Tron said. "She is. Her mother drove up from Louisville and dropped her off on Friday. She spent the weekend with me and is gonna be goin' back tomorrow when her mother get up here."

"Okay," Shawna said, clearly wanting to hear more – wanting to hear about this possible favor.

"And I was wonderin' if you would come through and see her," Tron said. "Look, baby...Shawna." He quickly corrected himself, knowing that she was not going to be okay with him calling her *baby* the way he had for all those years. It was still first reaction for him. "I know I fucked up," he began. "And I told you I'm sorry and stuff. And I know you know that I got her pregnant and shit. Trust me, I do not feel good about this shit, either. But, like I said, Ebony is here and she keeps askin' about you. With this little stay being for her birthday and for Valentine's Day, I ain't wanna tell her what really happened and that you don't even live here no more. I told her that you went outta town cause she keep askin' about you. So, I was just wonderin' if you could come thru either tonight or earlier in the day tomorrow and see her for a little bit. Say you gotta go somewhere tonight or something, she won't know the difference."

There was a long pause of dead silence on the phone. Tron could hear the silence, instantly starting to feel guilty for

55

even calling Shawna and asking her to help him out in any way.

"Shawna?" Tron asked.

"Yeah," Shawna said. "I'm here. Look, Tron, I hope you ain't try'na make this lead to nothin', cause I really am movin' on and passed all of this. I have been humiliated and embarrassed."

"I know you have," Tron said. "I know, Shawna. Like I said, I was just askin' for Ebony, that's all. I swear."

"Yeah," Shawna said. "I believe you, somehow. Look, I just got done with Miss Susan's hair. When I get done cleanin' up, I can come over there and see Ebony for a minute, if that would be okay with you."

"Yeah," Tron said, smiling a little bit. "That's fine. She been askin' about you, Shawna. She really has."

"Yeah," Shawna said, thinking about how she enjoyed basically playing the role of the little girl's stepmother. "I'll be over there within a hour or so, okay?"

"Okay," Tron said.

The two ended the call. When Tron sat his phone on the bed next to him, he went back to thinking. He felt relieved that Shawna was at least nice enough to come see Ebony before she left town.

Chapter 4

Desirae was pulling into a parking spot outside of her apartment building twenty minutes after leaving Tron's place. The entire drive across town, she played the scenario over in her mind of when she walked up to Tron and his daughter, Ebony. She also thought more and more about how he looked at her in that moment. To her, it was the look of disgust, among many other things.

"That nigga jus' gon look at me like I'm nothin'," Desirae said as she thought about it. Her head shook as she turned her car off and headed into her apartment.

Once inside, Desirae quickly slid out of her coat and sat down into her usual spot on the couch. She looked around her apartment, knowing that she would soon move out of this place and live with her mother again. On top of all that, she would be doing all of this with two babies. Her feelings and emotions were everywhere; her fears were on steroids.

Just then, Desirae could feel her phone vibrating in her pocket. It was her mother calling. In all honesty, she did not feel like talking to her mother right now. However, she could also see UNREAD MESSAGE alerts in the background on her phone screen. There was no doubt that her mother was calling her about what she had found out at the doctor. After taking a deep breath, Desirae answered the phone.

"Hello, Mama," Desirae answered. "Sorry I ain't call you back, just been dealin' with some stuff."

"Well, how are you?" Karen asked, talking softly. "I got the text message you sent me."

"Yeah," Desirae said. "The doctor pulled up the inside of my stomach and everything on the computer. I saw it with my own two eyes. She said that she won't be able to tell me the sex of the babies for a few more weeks or something like that, but I am definitely having twins."

"Well," Karen said, clearly sounding as if she was at a loss for words. "I can definitely say that you would be the first that I have known of in our family to have twins."

"Oh, great," Desirae said sarcastically. "That's just perfect, Mama."

"Look, Desirae," Karen said, sounding as if she was going into her motherly mode. "I know it's probably not the kind of news that you were planning to hear when you walked through those doors earlier. But there is no point in being down about it now. There is nothing that you can do to change this now."

"Yeah," Desirae said. "I know, I know. I'mma go ahead and start packin' today, when I feel like it. I'mma prolly lay up and take a nap or something."

"Yeah, well," Karen said. "Have you told your father yet? Did you call him? And what about this Tron person you speak of. Have you told him yet that it's twins?"

Desirae took a deep breath. "That's where I'm comin' from now, Mama," she said. "I just came from his place. And no, I did not tell daddy yet. I was over at Tron's, telling him."

"And?" Karen asked. "What did he say? Knowing how men are, he is probably going to try to say that you not pregnant by him. Some men can handle hearing that they're having one baby. But, baby, when you get to talking more than that, they get real scared all of the sudden."

"Yeah, well," Desirae said. "That's one way of puttin' it. He wasn't even answerin' my texts or calls when I left the doctor's office. I was just calling and trying to tell him that it was twins, since he didn't go to the doctor with me." Desirae remembered that she needed to keep the lie up with her mother. "I don't think he real happy about this."

"Well," Karen said. "Did he say that he was going to help you or what? I mean, I'm here for you, Desirae. And you know that I always will be. However, taking care of two babies at once is really going to put a strain on you, and your finances, once you have those again. Everything is going to have to cost twice as much. You do know that, right?"

"Yeah, Mama," Desirae answered, sounding a little annoyed. "I know, Mama. I know. And he said that he was gonna help me and stuff."

"Well," Karen said. "Let's just hope that he sticks to his word. Even if he doesn't, you already know what you gotta do. Carry your ass right on downtown and put him on child support. Don't be one of these women who says that they can do it on their own. Sure, you may be able to. And you won't be the first, nor will you be the last to do it. However, you want to try to make things as easy as you can with this...for you...not easy for him."

"Yeah, well," Desirae said. "I'mma do some more thinkin' about that. He offered to help me move and stuff this weekend, so that's something."

"Oh, okay," Karen said.

Karen could sense that her daughter was not in the best of moods. When she was calling her, Karen debated on what she would say. There was no doubt in her mind that there would be a lot of uncertainty on Desirae's end. Karen, herself, imagined the pressure a young, unmarried, unemployed woman must be under when she finds out that she is pregnant with not one, but two, babies.

"Well, I'll let you go," Karen said. "I was just calling to see how everything was going with you. You sound like you need a little rest. I'll just talk to you later on or tomorrow or something."

Desirae felt a little guilty – felt as if she was pushing her mother away a little bit. However, she knew that she would need a little time to herself. "Okay, Mama," Desirae said. "I'll talk to you later."

The two of them said bye to one another and Desirae sat her phone on the couch next to her. She looked down at her stomach, as she began to think about just how much her body would change now that she was carrying two babies. Did that mean that she would gain twice the weight? Did all of this mean that it would now be twice as hard for her to lose the weight after the pregnancy?

Desirae's thoughts turned to Reese. She could not even think about her former best friend without getting a sour taste in her mouth. The amount of betrayal was just too much to even stomach. However, at the same time, Desirae thought about how this would be one of those moments where she would jump on the phone and call Reese as quickly as she could to tell her the news. However, after talking to Reese earlier, she knew even more that she was nothing but a liar and that she was someone that could just not be trusted.

Desirae turned on the television, hating that she could not smoke a blunt or drink any wine right now. She knew that tonight would be a particularly sad night because it was Valentine's Day. Whatever other friends and cousins she had would be out with their boos, being in love and having a good time. What had she done today? She had found out that she was pregnant with twins, only to go over to their father and be insulted and basically treated as if she was nothing.

While the television played as background noise, Desirae logged into her Facebook and Instagram accounts. She could not help but smile at all of the comments she got from different dudes online. Routinely – about once every couple of weeks or so – she would upload a photo of herself in either a cute outfit or lying under sheets on her bed, naked. It never failed: she would always get comments of praise about her body. Dudes hollered at her left and right. After thinking about how Tron treated her like she was some ugly chick, she looked at some of the guys who hollered at her online. And some of them actually seemed to have their shit together, based on what she saw of their profiles. There were quite a few that had decent jobs, were handsome, posted pictures of nice cars, and, most importantly, appeared to be single.

"I don't even know why I was wastin' my time on that nigga," Shawna said, starting to feel angry. "I believed that shit he said about wanting to break it off with his girl and come and be with me. I actually believed it, when I coulda been gettin' with one of these dudes that would feel lucky to have me. Now look at me." Desirae looked down at her stomach. "Who gon' wanna date a bitch with two babies by some other nigga?"

Desirae set her phone back down, knowing that it was just too depressing to think about how her love life was going to change, let alone everything else. She really had slipped up and forgotten about taking her birth control. Hell, there were so many times that Tron came in her that she did not get pregnant that she just did not think much about it.

Desirae pulled a knitted blanket from the side of the couch. After spreading it across her body, she leaned back into the couch. The longer she sat there, thinking, she more she felt scorned and done wrong. There was just something about how Tron was talking to her and treating her that she could not let go of. Yes, she signed up for fucking around with him on the side, but she did not sign up for feeling invisible at the time when she needed to be seen the most. It would probably be safe to say that a sort of rage was brewing inside of her. And finding out that she was pregnant with twins only made it twice as strong.

***

Tron chilled out for a few minutes and smoked about a third of the blunt he had just rolled. Soon enough, he went back downstairs to hang out with Ebony. She talked to him about this and that, with somewhat long spurts of time when the only noise in the house was the television going. Within an hour or so, there was a knock at the door.

"Daddy, you hear that?" Ebony asked, looking at her father from her sprawled out spot on the floor. "Sound like somebody at the door."

Tron jumped up, knowing exactly who it would be at the door: Shawna. He hated that she even bothered to knock, because it could send a message to Ebony that Shawna did not live there anymore. Tron hurried across the living room floor and along the stairway until he got to the front door. He looked over his clothes quickly, making sure that he did not look crazy himself, before he pulled the front door open.

Instantly, Tron's eyes met with Shawna's. It felt so strange, to the both of them, having not seen one another for a couple of weeks.

"Wassup?" Tron said, not really knowing what to say. "How you?"

Shawna, not really wanting to make eye contact, looked away. "I'm okay," she said, flatly. "I'll be a lot better if I could come in out of the cold, Tron."

Immediately, Tron moved out of the way and allowed Shawna to enter.

"She still here, right?" Shawna asked, pulling her gloves then hat off.

Tron nodded, as he pushed the front door closed. "Yeah," he said. He then pointed toward the living room. "She in there, Shawna."

61

"Okay," Shawna said.

Shawna put her game face on – smiling as if she was actually happy to be there – and headed into the living room. Tron, still standing by the doorway, listened for a moment. Ebony jumped up off of the floor and hugged Shawna, telling her how much she missed her.

"Where did you go?" Ebony asked. "Daddy told me that you went outta town. Where did you go, Shawna?"

"Well," Shawna said, clearly caught off guard by the little girl's question. "I went a couple of places, actually. I'm staying with my sister to help her out for a minute, but your dad told me that you were asking about me."

"I did," Ebony said. "I did."

"Yeah," Shawna said. "So, that's why I decided to stop by and see you for a little bit."

Tron came into the room and the three of them hung out. Tron thanked his lucky stars that Ebony was too young to pick up on the tension between himself and Shawna. He also, silently, thanked Shawna for going along with this – for being woman enough to look passed him and step out a little bit for his daughter.

Shawna visited for about thirty minutes, never really getting too comfortable. Just as it was getting dark outside, she decided it was time to go.

"Well," Shawna said. "I gotta go back over to my sister's so I can help her, Ebony. Your dad told me that you were here and I wanted to see you so bad that I just couldn't help myself."

Ebony smiled and bear-hugged Shawna, telling her goodbye.

Tron walked Shawna to the door.

"Thank you so much for doin' this," Tron said, graciously. Not only was he thankful for Shawna coming by, but also that this visit would keep Ebony from thinking about Desirae. Last thing he needed was for her to dwell too much on Desirae, at least not for a while.

"Well, Tron," Shawna said. "I ain't do this for you. And I just want you to know that. I decided to come over because you said that Ebony was asking about me. And it's her birthday and Valentine's Day, or whatever."

"I know, Shawna," Tron said, looking down toward the floor. "I know."

Shawna could pick up on how down Tron was. After all, with the two of them being together for some years, she knew when something was up even when he was not going to say anything. Instead of asking what the issue was, Shawna slipped into her coat, put on her hat and gloves, and went on about her business.

When Shawna walked out of the door, Tron pushed the door closed behind her and stood there for a moment in thought. He really didn't know when he would see Shawna again. Even though he had really messed up, he wished deep down that this would not be the last time. He knew that she would never even consider getting back with him. And that was something that he would just have to live with.

Tron went back to the living room and sat back down onto the couch. The word *twins* continued to swirl around in his mind. All he could think about, and kind of hope for, was that there was a way that Desirae was not pregnant by him. He felt so stupid for accomplishing all he had accomplished – going from dealing drugs in the streets to owning a strip club – and yet allowing some THOT to get pregnant by him. From time to time, Tron thought about it so much that he would just shake his head.

***

Later that night, Tron put Ebony to bed in his bed and headed back downstairs. The two of them had eaten dinner together before watching a movie in the living room. Tron could see that his daughter was getting a little sleepy and nodding off during conversation, but he waited until she was good and sleep to turn the television off then carry her upstairs.

When Tron was settling himself on the couch, he heard keys jingling at the door. He jumped up, wide awake again. He rushed to the front door as Tyrese came in. His eyes were red, and he had a bit of a smirk on his face.

"Hey, wassup, man?" Tyrese said as he walked in the door.

"What you doin' here, nigga?" Tron asked, surprised to see Tyrese.

Tyrese looked at Tron. "What you mean what I'm doin' here, nigga?" he said back. "You told me that your daughter was goin' home Monday, didn't you?"

"Naw, nigga," Tron said. "I said she would be goin' home Tuesday, not Monday. She upstairs sleeping, so watch how loud you talk. I don't need your ass to go wakin' her up, cause then she'll be up all night."

"Oh," Tyrese said, turning back around. "My bad. I'll just come back tomorrow." He began to get his phone out to see what his options were as far as staying somewhere for the rest of the night.

"Naw, man, naw," Tron said. "You ain't gotta go right back out the door. Come in and chill for a sec, man. Ya boy done had a crazy day."

Tyrese put his phone away and followed Tron into the living room. "Word?" he said, wanting to hear more. "What you mean, Tron? Wassup?"

"Desirae," Tron answered, flatly. He then grabbed a magazine from the small table at the end of the couch. Earlier, when he had smoked some of the blunt, he put the remaining part inside of the magazine so it would not get broken. He opened the magazine, pulled the blunt out, grabbed a lighter, and then handed the two to Tyrese. "This some good shit," Tron said.

"Awe, fuck," Tyrese said. "What done happened now with her ole ratchet ass? What she do?"

"Man," Tron said, shaking his head from side to side. "She just gon' come stoppin' by earlier, when I was playin' outside with Ebony."

"Damn," Tyrese said. "Man, you need to move. All your hoes know where to find you, and come jump on you, I guess. Man, you need to just move. Why she stop by without callin'? What she want? Did she wanna come back through for a round two with try'na kill your ass with a fork?"

Tron looked at his boy with slanted eyes. "Nigga, you gon' stop makin' a joke about that shit," he warned.

Tyrese laughed and held his hands up. "Okay, okay," he said. "I'm bein' serious, though, man. What that chick want that she would just be poppin' up?"

"Bruh," Tron said. "I had seen her callin' and stuff, textin' me sayin' that she went to the doctor today. But I ain't answer cause I was hangin' out with Ebony and I ain't really feel like none of her bullshit."

"I know that's right," Tyrese said, handing the blunt to Tron. Tron grabbed it and took a long, hard hit. "But what she want though?" he asked. "I know she ain't just come all the way over here from where you said she live – out south? – to tell you that she went to the damn doctor today. There had to be something else, man. Had to be."

Tron allowed the weed to go to his head a little bit before he continued on with explaining.

"Man," Tron said. "She came over to tell me that when she went to the doctor today, she found out that she pregnant with twins."

Tyrese's eyes bulged. For a split second, he thought that he had misheard. "Tron, nigga," Tyrese said. "Are your serious? You got her pregnant with twins?"

Tron nodded his head, having just as hard of a time believing what he had just said as Tyrese was having heard it. "Yup," he said, very somberly. "The bitch went to the doctor and found out that she was pregnant with fuckin' twins."

"Damn, man," Tyrese said, trying to hold back a snicker. "What the fuck you gon' do, nigga? Two fuckin' babies?"

"What you mean what the fuck I'mma do?" Tron said. He then shrugged his shoulders. "Man, I don't even know what I'mma do. I still can't believe this shit. I really think that bitch did this shit on purpose."

"On purpose?" Tyrese asked. "How the fuck you mean she did this shit on purpose? How a woman gon' purposely choose to have twins and shit? That don't even make sense."

"Nigga, you stupid," Tron said. "I ain't talkin' bout the twin part of this situation, you dummy. I'm talkin' bout the fact that she got pregnant. I think she did that stuff on purpose. I think she purposely stopped takin' her birth control so that she could get pregnant by me. I brought it up, but of course she said that she didn't."

"Well, duh, nigga," Tyrese said, as if it all was obvious. "You and me both know that. I knew that the second you told me – that she got pregnant on purpose. That's how some of them side chicks be, especially when they see that you got something that they wish they had, like a relationship."

"Yeah," Tron said. He nodded his head and thought about what his boy Tyrese was saying to him.

"Man, that's why I never tell'em that I got another chick," Tyrese said. "That's how bitches wind up jealous. And you know how jealous women be actin' – like they ain't got no damn sense. Plus, man, you shoulda been usin' a condom so they couldn't even come up with this *I'm pregnant* bullshit. You opened the door for this shit, in some ways, your damn self."

"Man, I told her when we first started hookin' up that she needed to be on birth control," Tron said. "Cause them condoms just be too fuckin' tight for a nigga. They too fuckin' tight and shit."

"I know what you mean," Tyrese said, shaking his head. "But, still man. Maybe you should have pulled out rather than nuttin' in her shit... I don't know. I'm just glad that it ain't me in that kinda situation."

"Well, good," Tron said, handing the blunt back to Tyrese. "I'm glad. It's good that you happy that you not in this situation."

Tyrese picked up on his boy Tron's sarcastic tone and shook his head. "Nigga, don't be sittin' over there gettin' shitty with me and shit," he said. "I told you how to handle your hoes, but you just wouldn't listen."

"Nigga, shut up," Tron said. "You the one who had a chick get shot at and shit in the back of the club, let's not forget that shit."

"I can forget that shit all I want," Tyrese said. "I ain't get the crazy bitch pregnant. You gon' have to see that chick Desirae for the rest of your life, or at least for eighteen years. I'm just glad it ain't me, I swear I am."

"Yeah, yeah," Tron said, just ready for the conversation to move on. "I know, I know. Hold up, nigga. What you come walkin' through the door with a smile on your face and shit for? Why the fuck was you so happy?"

"Man, I met this chick," Tyrese told Tron. "This thick chick over on the west side. I met her online and all she was talkin' bout is how she wanna suck some dick and shit. So, I hit her up. I like the pics and shit and she ask me for a pic of my shit, you know? So, I took a picture of my dick and sent it to her. Man, the rest is history. Next thing I know, I'm parked outside of this house she stay in, over offa Tibbs. I think she stay with her family or something. I'm tellin' you, though. She got these big ass lips. When I saw that face pic, a nigga couldn't wait to stick his dick in that mouth. Like I said, next thing I know, I'm over parked outside of her place and she is slobbin' my dick like the bitch ain't ate in days."

Tron began to zone out a little bit as he listened to the details of Tyrese's encounter. Sure, some good head would definitely help him feel better at that moment. However, hearing that he was possibly having twins with Desirae just ruined his entire spirit – even the weekend he spent with Ebony couldn't repair it.

"Man, I got a lot on my mind," Tron had to come on out and say. "I think that she either trapped me or done got pregnant by some other nigga and is just try'na use me for a meal ticket."

"Shit," Tyrese said. "Wouldn't surprise me. You know these hoes ain't loyal. You know how these hood chicks be schemin' dudes to help them take care of a baby that ain't even theirs. And, to make matters worse, if you get in too deep with taking care of the child and helping to raise it and find out later on that the kid ain't even yours, these court systems will make a nigga pay child support for a kid that ain't even his...for a kid that don't even belong to him."

"I know," Tron said. "I know."

"Did you ask for a paternity test?" Tyrese asked.

"Yes and no," Tron said. "I definitely let her know that I wasn't even sure if the baby was mine. But you can imagine how that went. She took that as me callin' her a hoe."

"Well, damn nigga," Tyrese said. "Ain't that what she is. You said it yourself that she was just something to fuck and suck on your dick. She the one that took it a step further by not being on birth control like any other grown ass chick out here should be."

"Exactly, nigga," Tron said. "That's what I'm sayin. But, for some reason, I can tell that she was really wantin' more and shit. Like she was wantin' for us to be together or somethin'."

"Nigga, I don't care what you say," Tyrese said. "She ain't just get that shit from nowhere. You musta planted that shit in her mind for her to even think comin' up to the club, and y'all bein' together, would even be a fuckin' option. I told you what to do, nigga. I swear, I don't even have these kinds of problems."

"Yeah, yeah," Tron said, wanting his boy to stop pointing that sort of thing out. "Well, I gotta deal with this problem now."

Tyrese snickered. "Just wait," he said. "Once she really get into this pregnancy, and her hormones make her start actin' all crazy, you really gon' see the bitch act up. You betta be findin' out as quick as possible if she even pregnant by you or if she ain't. I'm tellin' you, nigga. These hoes ain't loyal."

Chapter 5

The next morning, Desirae woke up from what felt like a long nap, even though she had probably slept for around eight hours, and slid out of bed. Quickly, she made her way to the bathroom. For the umpteenth time, she looked at her body in the mirror. However, this morning was the first morning that she knew she was having two babies instead of just one. She had begun to think of everything through different lenses since finding out.

"I'mma do it today," Desirae said to herself. Last night, she had decided that she was going to call her father today. Since the divorce, she did not really see her father as much as she did when she was growing up. And she was happy for that. Desirae already knew that her father viewed her as being fast and a little too loose. He had said a couple of things to her over the years that let her know her father just did not know what kind of chick she was. Nonetheless, he was always there for her. And she could not deny that.

Desirae sat on her couch and called her father, knowing that even though he was from the streets, he was definitely more of a morning kind of person.

"Hello," Desirae's father, George, said. His voice was a little groggy.

"Hey, Daddy," Desirae said. "It's Desirae."

Immediately, George woke up. He sounded as if he was leaning up in his bed. "Awe, hey, baby," he said. "How you been?"

"I been good, Daddy," Desirae answered. "I been good." She looked down at her stomach. "How you been? What you been up to?"

"Awe, not too much," George answered. "Just been working. Me and a couple buddies went to Chicago. Almost got caught up in some shit on the south side with these niggas outside of this restaurant, but we made it out. So, I can say that I had a little fun." He laughed. "When you gon' come up and see me? You supposed to, remember you told me that? Don't go actin' like you done forgot a nigga now."

Desirae giggled. She did in fact remember promising her father that she was going to see him. She could not

69

remember why she had been putting off. First, it seemed like she was talking to this guy, then that guy. Then, next thing she knew, she was involved with Tron – at the phone every time he called; fresh to meet when he walked through the door.

"I don't know, Daddy," Desirae answered. "I called, partly, cause I got something to tell you."

"Awe, shit," George said. "What is it? What you got to tell me?"

"Well," Desirae said. It was so hard to not hesitate. She felt even more nervous telling her father than she did her mother. She knew that her father did not see her as a little angel. However, Desirae also knew that any man who had taken the time to be a father would probably not want his daughter to wind up getting pregnant by some nigga who don't even want to acknowledge her. "Daddy…" she said. "I'm pregnant."

There was a brief pause – a pause that caused Desirae to bite her lip with anticipation. She wondered what her father was thinking on the other end. She knew that he would try to play it cool. However, after he got through his cool phase, his true feelings and opinions would start to make themselves known. That was the part that Desirae was not looking forward. And with news like this, that moment in time could come even sooner. She looked up at the ceiling, as if she was looking into Heaven and talking to God. She only asked that her father did not ask certain questions. *Good God*, she thought. *There are just some things I don't wanna talk about with Daddy. Please!*

"Awe, okay," George said. He clearly sounded as if he was at a loss for words. "Congratulations, baby. How far along are you, and when are you due?"

Desirae calmed down for a second, liking how her father was responding to the news so far. "Well," she began. "I'm like three months pregnant. So, I'm due in late August or early September. I went to the doctor for the first time, yesterday."

"Oh, yeah?" George said. "Well, that's good."

Now, Desirae could hear her father's tone changing. He truly did sound like he had just heard something he did not want to hear.

"I gotta ask," George said, sounding as if he was coming to a crossroads. "Who are you pregnant by, Desirae? Who is the child's father?"

Desirae bit her bottom lip and looked up toward the ceiling. She felt as if God was not listening to her, as this particular question was one that she hoped her father would not ask just yet.

"His name is Tron," Desirae answered. "And, like I was sayin', I went to the doctor yesterday for the first time. Not only am I due in late August and early September, but I am also pregnant with twins."

"Twins!" George said. "Baby, is you serious? Twins?"

"Yes, Daddy," Desirae said. "As in two babies."

Desirae's mother's words of wisdom about how men act when they find out that a woman is pregnant with two babies popped into her mind. She almost wanted to laugh at how on point her mother could be at times.

"Oh, okay," George said. Desirae could visualize him shaking his head. "Well," he said. "About this Tron, Desirae. How long you been seein' the nigga? Why I ain't met him or heard about him? Who the fuck is the nigga?"

Desirae took a deep breath then swallowed, feeling a little nervous even though she was talking on the phone and her father lived a couple of hours away. "I told you, Daddy," Desirae told him. "His name is Tron. And you ain't met him cause, you know, we wasn't really like that, you know."

"No, I don't know," George said. "Tell me what I'm supposed to know. Who the fuck is this nigga that got my daughter pregnant? That's all I wanna know."

"Daddy," Desirae said, being a little more forceful. "Don't go try'na make this any harder for me, please. I told you that his name is Tron."

"Okay," George said, getting the point. His daughter was trying to not go into too many details with him. He had been around the block enough to know that this tactic meant

71

that she really didn't want to say who Tron really is. "Have you told him about the babies and stuff?"

"Yeah," Desirae answered. "I did."

"So, are y'all gon' be like together and stuff?" George asked. "I'm not mad, Desirae. I just wanna understand, is all. I swear, I ain't mad."

Desirae decided to let her guard down. Strangely enough, because her father had lived a bit more than her mother and he was not so refined, she felt like she could relate to him better.

"No," Desirae said, sounding somewhat disappointed. "It was never like that, Daddy. You know what I mean. We was just, you know, kickin' it."

"Desirae," George said. "Is this a married man you pregnant by?"

"No, Daddy," Desirae responded. "Naw. He ain't married. In fact, he single now."

"Oh, okay," George said. "Well, let me ask you this then: What does the nigga do for a living? How the nigga make his money?"

Desirae closed her eyes and hyperventilated. This, again, was another question that she prayed to God that her father would not ask her. She thought that she could lie, but she knew that keeping up with the lie, especially with her Daddy, would be too much to do when the two saw one another again.

"He owns a club, Daddy," Desirae said.

"Awe, fuck," George said. It sounded as if the words slipped out of his mouth, without any sort of filter. "He own a fuckin' club? Is that where you met the nigga, Desirae? In the club? What kinda club is this? Where is it at?"

"Daddy, why do all that matter?" Desirae asked. "And, no, I ain't meet him in no club. He just so happen to own a club, is all I said."

"Cause," George said. "I just want you to understand what you may have gotten yourself into. That club business ain't nothin' to fuck around with. I ain't sayin' you had to go get the guy downtown in a business suit. But I did want you to stay away from drug dealers and niggas who be up in the club

72

all the time and shit. I'm tellin' you, don't nothin' good come outta that shit."

Desirae did not want to say the name of the club, nor where it was. She knew that even though her father had moved away from Indianapolis since the divorce, he still had an ear in the streets, so to speak. He was still very much in touch with certain people he had either ran the streets with or worked with. And if she said the name *Honeys East*, she was sure that her father would have at least heard of it. It makes the news enough in Indianapolis that other parts of Indiana could very well hear about the place.

"He make good money, Daddy," Desirae said. "So don't you worry about it."

"Desirae," George said. "I just wanna know what kinda nigga got my daughter pregnant. That's all. Why you don't wanna tell me about this club that he own? How old is he?"

"He like my age, maybe a year or so older," Desirae explained.

"And the nigga own a fuckin' club already?" George asked. "Where the fuck he get the money to do some shit like that? What he do to get that kinda money at such a young age?"

This was a question that Desirae herself did not even have an answer for.

"I don't know, Daddy, damn," Desirae said, feeling frustrated. "I don't know."

"What you mean you don't know?" George asked. "You pregnant by the nigga, ain't you?"

"Yeah, Daddy, but I don't know," Desirae said.

"Oh, okay," George said. "Well, maybe I'll have to come down and meet this Tron nigga real soon. Maybe this weekend or something."

"Daddy," Desirae said. "Have you talked to Mama lately?"

"Naw," George answered. "I ain't talked to her lately. Why? Why you ask that? I know she gave you a good talkin' to when you told her about this."

"Yeah," Desirae said. She then smirked just thinking about it. "Yeah, she did just that, all right. But, no, I was asking

73

because this weekend I'm supposed to be moving in with Mama again. I'm not workin' right now."

"You not workin'?" George asked, clearly surprised. "What you mean you not workin'? I thought you was workin' up at some department store in the mall or something. What the fuck happened with that?"

"Long story," Desirae said, definitely not wanting to go there with her father. "Long story, Daddy. Not right now."

"Oh, okay," George said. "So, you said you movin' back in with your mama this Friday? Who supposed to be helpin' you do that shit? Huh? Maybe I should come down there then and you could arrange a little meetin' for me and this Tron nigga. I ain't try'na scare him off or nothin'. I just wanna meet the nigga...see where his head is at and shit, you know?"

"I don't know, Daddy," Desirae said, shaking her head. Things were so shaky as it was with her and Tron that she did not want to make things worse. "I don't know."

"Well, who you got helpin' you move?" George asked.

"Nobody right now," Desirae answered. "You know that Mama will be at work. I texted a couple friends and am waitin' to hear back."

"Awe, yeah?" George said. "Well, I'll tell you this. This Friday, I can head down there when I get up and help you at whatever point you're at. If you're already done moving by the time I get down there, we can go eat somewhere or somethin' – catch up and shit."

Desirae smiled. "Okay, Daddy," she said. She then let out a deep breath. "I already know you gon' be down here early in the morning so you can have more time to pick my brain about Tron and stuff."

"Naw," George said. "I'm not. I promise. I'mma just come help you move."

Desirae did not believe a word that was coming out of her father's mouth. Knowing him, he would be knocking at her door at no later than ten o'clock.

"Yeah, whatever," Desirae said. "You'll be here around ten."

"Around ten?" George asked. "In the morning? Baby, I ain't young no more. I may be up that early, but I definitely ain't gon be all the way down the highway a couple of hours yet. I'll get there when I get there. You can go on and do whatever you gon' do, baby. And when I get there, we'll just go from there. Okay?"

"Yeah," Desirae said. "That's coo, I guess. That's coo."

Just then, Desirae could hear in the background what sounded like a couple of women walking through her father's door. Desirae already knew what that meant, remembering why he and her mother's marriage had fallen to pieces.

"Okay, then," George said. "Well, I'm bout to head out and get my day started."

"Hmm, hmm," Desirae said, suspicious of the noise in the background. "I'll talk to you later, Daddy. Don't do nothin' I wouldn't do."

"Yeah," George said. "I'll keep that in mind."

Desirae said goodbye to her father and hung up the phone. Now, she sat alone, once again, in the living room of her apartment. Everything was so silent. And she was rather pleased with how her father handled the news that she was pregnant. She started to think of ways that she could talk her father out of coming down to Indianapolis to help her move. She decided that she would give herself a couple of days before totally deciding.

***

On Tuesday afternoon, Tron sat parked in the parking lot of Honeys East. He was so antsy to get his daughter back into the hands of her mother. There was some business that he needed to handle, and Andria being later than she had said to pick Ebony up was just not working for him. Tyrese was already there and had gone inside. There was no doubt in Tron's mind that Tyrese would be inside, smashing some thick booty stripper like there was no tomorrow.

Tron focused on the parking lot entrance, waiting to see Andria's car swoop into the parking lot. "Dammit, where is she?" he said out loud.

Ebony, in the backseat, heard. "Is that Mommy?" she asked, not really knowing what her father had said.

This morning, when the two of them had woken up, Tron took Ebony to get some breakfast at Hardees. After they

75

ate, he took her to the mall so she could get some more clothes. She now had at least five outfits and three new pairs of shoes.

"No, Ebony," Tron said, looking down at his phone. "It ain't her. She ain't here yet." Tron held his phone up to the side of his face, calling Andria.

Within a few rings, Andria answered. "Hello?" she said, sounding a little aggravated.

"Are you close or what?" Tron asked. "I got a meeting I gotta be at and you said that you was gon' be here already."

"Damn," Andria said. "I got stuck in some traffic, Tron. I'mma be there in like five minutes. I'm comin' up on downtown right now."

"Okay," Tron said. "Whatever. I'll see you when you get here."

The two ended the call without even saying goodbye. Tron pushed his head back into the headrest of his seat. The next few minutes actually passed rather smoothly. Next thing Tron and Ebony knew, Andria came rolling up into the parking lot. She slid into a parking spot as Ebony began to unbuckle her seatbelt.

"Finally," Tron said to himself, almost whispering.

Tron climbed out of his seat then helped Ebony out of her seat. He walked her over to Andria's car. After he hugged Ebony and the two talked about how much fun they'd had together and when they might be going on that trip they talked about, Ebony got into the car and closed the door. Tron approached Andria's window.

"How was your weekend?" Tron asked, sounding nice.

"My weekend was fine," Andria answered suspiciously. "Why?"

"I can't ask about your weekend?" Tron asked.

Andria squinted at Tron. "What the fuck are you getting at? What do you want?" she asked.

Tron leaned up, looking down at the mother of his child with eyes that let her know that he was just not in the mood for her attitude right now. "Please, not right now," he said to her. "So, anything you wanna tell me about that might be coming up that I should know about?"

Andria thought about it for a minute, trying to figure out what he was asking. She shrugged. "Not that I can think of," she answered, flatly. "What are you talkin' bout, Tron?"

"Eric," Tron said. "That's who I'm talkin' bout. So, you got you some new dude that you might be movin' in with and with my child, huh?"

Andria slammed her head back into the seat and rolled her eyes. She then looked at Ebony in the rearview mirror, shaking her head. "I told her ass not to tell you," Andria said, quietly. "Anyway, Tron, yeah. I've gotten to the point to where maybe I wanna move on. Shit, you have. You moved in with a chick and everything. So why can't I?"

"I ain't say that you couldn't, Andria," Tron said. "I was just askin' when was you gon' tell me since my daughter would be livin' with this nigga too."

"Shit, I don't know," Andria said. "I ain't even thought that far ahead yet to really be knowin' all that. What, you wanna meet him or somethin'?"

"Well, don't you think that I should?" Tron asked.

"Fuck," Andria said. "I don't know. Look, I ain't really up for talkin' about all this right now. Let me go on and get back down to Louisville before it starts snowing again. I can call you and tell you if you really feel like that you need to know."

Tron nodded, stepping back from Andria's car. "Okay, okay," he said. He realized that he was probably going a little too hard, especially considering the situation, or situations, that he had going in his own life. Tron waved bye to Ebony in the backseat as he headed toward the back of the building. Once he got inside and walked down the back hallway, he stepped up to the door of Tyrese's office, to see if he could hear anything. He didn't, so he went ahead and knocked.

"Nigga," Tron said. "I'm done with my kid. Her mama came and picked her up."

Just then, Tron could hear moaning noises – and the moaning was not a woman, but rather his boy Tyrese. The slurping noises were unmistakable, and he knew that Tyrese was getting his dick sucked. He snickered and shook his head, amazed at how Tyrese kept a little THOT on deck to use at any given moment of the day.

"Be out there in a minute!" Tyrese announced. "Just gimme five more minutes...fuck."

"Aight, nigga," Tron said, heading back to his office. "Aight."

When Tron got back to his office, he sat in his chair and checked over some emails on the computer. He then did his usual Google search for Honeys East, just to see what came up and if any people in the city were actively talking about the club online. Furthermore, he wanted to see what they would be saying. Luckily for Tron, for once, there did not appear to be a lot of chatter going on online. He was relieved to find this.

Within several minutes, Tron heard Tyrese's office door swing open. Words were exchanged between Tyrese and some woman before there was what sounded like a slap on her ass then a giggle. Tron shook his head. The chick – a thick booty girl, just like Tron thought out in the parking lot, went walking by Tron's office door. She smiled as she passed by and went out into the parking lot.

"Aight, nigga," Tron said as Tyrese stepped up to his office door. "You done with the hoes now or what?"

"Yeah, nigga," Tyrese said, buckling his belt. "Damn that shit was good. Naw, that shit wasn't good. That shit was fire."

"Yeah," Tron said, thinking of how the girl's mouth looked when she passed by his office. "She did look like she could suck some dick."

"I can get her back in here for you, nigga," Tyrese told him. "If you need some head, she will drop right down to her knees and suck on it real good. She try'na dance here, but she gon' have to work on that body a little bit first. Then, we can talk. Until then, though, I'mma see what other skills she got."

"Man, is all you do is fuck?" Tron asked. "Is that all you do? All you ever talk about is fuckin'."

"You one to talk," Tyrese said in response.

"Whatever, nigga," Tron said as he stood up. "I talked to the contractor dude on my way over here and he told me that we can finish everything up with remodeling the building as soon as the weather breaks. He said something about how

78

there was a lot of work that they could do in the cold, but all this snow makes it a different story."

"Right, right," Tyrese said, nodding his head. "Well, I was thinkin' that maybe we could think about redoing the lines in the parking lot. You know that we already can't halfway see that shit no way when there ain't even no snow on the ground. Plus, you know some of these niggas come in here some nights and come up to me complaining about the parking. Whoever had this building before us really fucked up out there cause when I was out there lookin', with how them lines are painted, it do seem like we could get more cars in the lot if we rearranged the lines."

Tron nodded as he wrote some of this down. "Aight, aight," he said, liking what he was hearing. "I think that is doable too. That's something that we could do."

Tron suggested that the two of them go out into the parking lot to look at the lines. They both had the idea of figuring out how many parking spots they could get in the parking lot if the lines were rearranged and repainted. As they stood out in the parking lot, talking, a car swooped in off of the street and into the lot. At first, they had just assumed that whoever was driving the car was using the lot to get back to the alley. However, they quickly saw that this was not the case. The car pulled into a parking spot, and a woman got out of the car.

"Why this chick look familiar?" Tyrese said, out loud.

Tron looked at her as she got closer to them and realized that this chick was the chick who was inside the club a couple of weeks back – the chick that Desirae had said was her best friend. What did she want?

Within a matter of seconds, Desirae's former best friend, Reese, was standing near Tron and Tyrese. She smiled, obviously nervous about even being there.

"Tron?" she said.

Tron nodded. "Yeah," he said. "Wassup?"

Tyrese looked at his boy Tron. He tried his hardest to hold back his laughter. In all reality, he wanted to just shake his head at all of the drama that Tron had going. Tyrese sort of remembered seeing this chick, but did not think he would be seeing her again anytime soon. He sort of just stepped back to allow her to say whatever she needed to say to Tron. Tron noticed, wishing that Tyrese would just stay where he was.

"I just wanted to talk to you about that night," Reese said. "I been feelin' guilty about it and shit."

Tron looked Reese up and down. While she did not have a body that was anywhere close to Desirae's body, she did have a nice face. She also came across as having a very nice personality. Since there had been virtually little to no interaction between the two of them the night that Desirae stabbed him with the fork, Tron had not really had the chance to form an impression of her. It was nice, though, that a woman was stepping to him to apologize, for once.

"Sorry for what?" Tron asked, showing a little bit of a smile. "What you got to feel sorry for?"

"Well," Reese said. "You know I'm Desirae's friend, Reese, and she always talked about you, and I know that me coming up here that night is what really made her go off the way she did."

"Oh, yeah?" Tron said, trying to understand it all. "I don't know if I would say that."

Tron could pick up on the way that Reese was looking at him. She constantly looked in his eyes, but in a way that was not THOT-ish. Rather, she seemed more like the kind of chick that a dude would take home to meet his mama.

Tyrese disappeared as Tron stood outside, talking to Reese.

"Look," Tron said, noticing that this Reese chick was obviously cold. "Let's step inside for a minute so we can talk or whatever."

Reese nodded and they walked around to the back of the building. Once inside, they sat across from one another in Tron's office. The building was so quiet. Tron had no idea where Tyrese had gone, and he did not think that he would have found a chick to come through that quick for a round two.

"Desirae," Reese began. "has been my best friend forever, but, well, you know how she is."

"Do I?" Tron said, feeling a little bitter. "I know she did this shit on purpose...Got pregnant by a nigga on purpose."

Reese shook her head. "Well," she said. "I don't know if she did it on purpose. I mean, she never said anything about doing something like that with me, so I don't know. I can't really speak on that."

Tron nodded. "Interesting," he said. He was beginning to wonder why this girl was here, in his face. What did she really want? What did she want that night when she was chilling off to the side out on the floor?

"Yeah," Reese said. She noticed how good Tron looked even when he was just wearing normal street clothes. For the last few days, she took different ways to get places around the city just so she could ride by the club. She was waiting for the chance to see Tron's car in the parking lot or something so that she could have a chance to talk to him. Some of the hurtful things that her former best friend had said to her yesterday only reminded her of just how much Desirae used to flaunt her looks and body in her face. "I mean, so I was comin' up here that night to talk to you because my friend, well, ex-friend, is just crazy. I don't know why she be actin' the way she act, and I was just comin' up here to let you know. I don't wanna see no chick do a man wrong the way Desirae do."

"Well," Tron said, standing up. "Thanks, but you a little late. I shoulda never messed around with that bitch. She always keep some shit goin'."

"Yeah," Reese said, her eyes focusing on the fly of Tron's pants. "She do... She do be actin' like that."

Tron looked down at Reese, noticing that she had a little bit of a figure. She also looked like she came for more than just talking to him. He had dealt with women enough to know that.

"She..." Tron said, his words trailing off as he shook his head. "That chick... She knew what she was doin'. She knew."

"Why you mess around with her if you know she crazy?" Reese asked. "All the dudes always want her and she be actin' so crazy with them that it just don't make no sense to me."

"It's complicated," Tron said, trying to think of what he could say to a comment like that. "She knew what I was lookin' for and she had to go doin' some dumb shit to change it. Now everybody is all fucked up. I swear." Tron shook his head. "I shoulda never fucked around with that shit and I wouldn't be in this frustrated situation. Don't blame yourself, though, for what happened that night. She the one who went off and got to stabbin' niggas with forks. She the one who got into it with my girl up at the mall." Tron was getting angry just thinking about Desirae.

Reese could see the anguish in Tron's eyes – anguish that Desirae had caused, being the bratty chick that she always had been. Just then, Reese stood up and pushed the office door almost closed. She could not take it anymore. Tron had to be one of the most handsome dudes she had ever met. She actually began to think about how Desirae signed up for something with him then, basically, went back on her word.

Tron watched her as she came closer to him.

"I'm sorry that she make you feel that way," Reese said, feeling nervous. She had never really had a chance to be alone with this kind of guy. "I really am. I know you gotta be frustrated and stuff with how she be actin', then she getting' pregnant by you."

"Yeah," Tron said, taking a deep breath. "She...She." He shook his head. "She sure know how to make a nigga life even harder."

Reese built up the courage to reach out and touch Tron's bulge. Through his pants, his manhood felt heavy. Tron, confused but not wanting to stop anything, just stood there.

"I got somethin' you wanna see?" Tron asked, knowing exactly what was going on. He knew that Desirae had talked about him to her best friend and now that very same friend was down in his office trying to jump on his dick. Normally, out of respect, he would avoid this kind of messiness and not do anything with the best friend of a chick he was fucking around with. However, now that Desirae had just fucked him over in several different ways, Tron just didn't give a fuck. In fact, he wanted to mess with this Reese chick even more now.

Reese smiled and grabbed his bulge harder, feeling it slowly getting a little bigger. "Maybe," she answered, wondering how big Tron's dick really was. "I mean... Do you got something that you wanna show me?"

Tron chuckled, glancing away then back at Reese's clear thirst for what he was packing in his pants. He sized her up quickly, trying to see if she just might have the skills to suck on his dick and do it right.

"If you wanna see it," Tron said. "You gotta get on your knees."

Reese, not even turning around to make sure that the door was closed, just about had stars in her eyes. Quickly, without even thinking, she lowered herself to her knees right in front of Tron. Her hands gripped the sides of his thighs and she waited, in anticipation, for him to finish unbuckling his belt and fly. When he did, he pulled his pants down to his knees. When his meat came free of the grip of his boxer briefs, it sprung forward, almost hitting Reese in the chin. Reese smiled as she grabbed it.

"Damn this is big," Reese said, stroking it. She now knew why her girl Desirae was making a fool of herself for this man. This was the biggest dick that Reese had ever seen.

Tron chuckled. "You like that shit?"

Reese kissed the head. "Hmm, hmm," she answered.

"Well," Tron said, thinking of how much this would get back at Desirae. "Don't just keep on lookin' at it. Suck that dick."

With no hesitation, Reese took Tron into her mouth. He even tasted good to her. Tron looked down and smiled at Reese's head, bobbing up and down his shaft, as she was clearly having the time of her life slobbing on him. To Tron, she looked so excited, as if she had never seen a dick before. He simply stood with his feet shoulder-width apart, his pants down at his knees, and allowed her to have her way.

"Yeah," Tron said, thinking about Desirae and how she had been actin' toward him. Now her own best friend was in his office and suckin' on his dick. "Suck that dick," Tron said, rubbing Reese's head. "Just suck on it...yeah."

Chapter 6

After Desirae got off the phone with her father, she took a little time to herself. About an hour or so later, she was up and moving about her apartment. She pulled stuff out of cabinets and cleared out closets so that she could pack things up before the last minute. Later that afternoon, she realized she needed to make a trip to the store. Desirae threw on some clothes and headed to the closest Walmart.

Inside, Desirae grabbed a shopping cart and casually looked around the store for this and that. As she was heading out of the store, after checking out, she noticed that Tron's old chick, Shawna, was coming out of the doors at the other end of the building. In fact, she was even walking toward the very same parking aisle as Desirae. It really is a small world, no matter where you live.

Desirae forced a smile, realizing that there was no point in getting into it with Shawna in the parking lot of a Walmart. She had already been embarrassed at Clarkes, then made to look like a fool up at Honeys East. She just couldn't keep doing that to herself, no matter how shitty she felt or how Tron treated her.

Shawna looked at Desirae. The two said *hey* as they came to the same parking aisle.

"How you been?" Shawna asked, deciding to be the bigger, more mature person. Even though she and Desirae had sort of come together to jump on Tron's ass that one time at the townhouse, she still had somewhat of a guard up when it came to this chick Desirae.

"Oh, I'm okay," Desirae said, not even really trying to make eye contact. "Just doin' me and shit now, you know?"

"Yeah," Shawna said, nodding her head. "I understand what you mean."

"I can't believe what that nigga did to me...to us," Desirae said, shaking her head. "I swear, these niggas don't be no good. None of them."

"Yeah," Shawna said. She then started to think about how good of a lie Tron had kept going. And how he had kept it going for so long. "You just never really know, do you?"

"Have you talked to him?" Desirae asked. The two of them were walking up to the rear of her car. "I mean, do you talk to him?"

"I ain't got shit I need to say to Tron," Shawna let Desirae know. "I saw him yesterday, but that was only because he called me, askin' me if I would come over to see his daughter while she was here. And I only did that because that little girl is so sweet, I just ain't wanna let her down."

"Yeah, she did seem like a nice little girl," Desirae said. "I met her yesterday, myself."

"Oh, really?" Shawna asked. "I didn't know that he had you come over there to meet his daughter. Okay."

"Well," Desirae said. "That's not really how it all happened. I was on my way home from the doctor and he was ignorin' my calls and my texts and shit. I got about halfway home and decided to turn my ass around and see if he was at home cause I really needed to talk to him. He was outside playin' with his little girl, so that's how I met her."

Shawna nodded and glanced at Desirae's stomach. "Okay," she said. "I see."

"Look," Desirae said, softly. "I know you don't really know me, and you probably don't want to because of how we met and all, but I'm kinda feelin' bad that I fell for this shit. I can't believe that I was coo with just bein' a nigga's side chick and now I'm the one who is gon' have to take care of these babies."

"Babies?" Shawna said, noticing that Desirae had used the plural form of the word. "You pregnant with more than one?"

Desirae nodded, glancing away. "Yeah," she said. "That's what I found out yesterday, and that was what I was wanting to tell Tron. I found out that I was pregnant with twins."

"Oh, wow," Shawna said. "Damn. Well, congratulations."

"Yeah, thanks," Desirae said, totally unenthused.

Shawna then thought of Tron, as she got really comfortable out in this Walmart parking lot. "So, what did Tron have to say about that, if you don't mind me askin'?" she asked.

"What don't he think?" Desirae responded, in a rhetorical sense. "That nigga think that I was out there fuckin' around and shit. He was sayin' some shit like he want a paternity test or somethin' to even know if I am really pregnant by his ass or not."

Shawna shook her head. "That don't make no damn sense," she said. The idea to ask Desirae about birth control popped into her mind, but she decided to not bring it up. In fact, she even went so far as deciding that whatever Desirae's response would be about birth control would be totally irrelevant. "Can I ask you somethin'?"

Desirae looked at Shawna, now finding a way to respect her feelings about this entire situation. "Sure," she said, shrugging her shoulders. "What is it?"

"If you knew that Tron belonged to someone and even lived with her and all that, why did you think bein' his girlfriend on the side was okay?" Shawna asked. As she asked this question, she was also thinking of Ms. Susan and her *love interest*, for lack of a better phrase, that lived down the highway in Ohio. "I mean, why do women think that that is okay? I just want to know. I'm not mad, at you, anyway, at this point. I just want to know."

Desirae pushed her cart between her car and the car next to her then leaned against the trunk. "Well," she explained, not even really knowing the answer to that question herself. "I don't know. I mean…I guess you think that maybe one day he is gonna choose you or somethin'. Maybe you think that you'll just be okay if you don't get too attached. Then, next thing you know, you are attached and you feel like you just as much of a girlfriend as the chick he had first. But, I don't really know how to explain it to you. I mean… every chick is different, probably. And I guess that I probably thought that fuckin' around with him on the side wasn't as bad because the nigga wasn't married."

Shawna nodded, finding what Desirae was saying to her interesting. "So," Shawna asked, "Is Tron talking about being involved and stuff? Are you sure that you even want to be bothered with him after all of this?"

"Hell naw, I don't wanna be bothered with his ass," Desirae said. "But, I'mma have to be, I guess. I mean, I can't take care of these two babies on my own, especially now. Ain't like I got no job or nothin' so that I can take care of them on my own. Shit, I'm movin' back in with my mama this weekend so I don't run through what little money I do got."

"I feel you on that," Shawna said.

"Now, let me ask you somethin'," Desirae said. "Do Tron take care of his daughter, Ebony, or whatever her name is? Do he do for her like a man supposed to do for his kids?"

Shawna thought about it for a second. "I mean..." she started. "He do and he don't. Ever since I had been with him, he always stayed on top of that child support. So, I know that that will not be a problem. I think his problem is prolly gonna be more-so with spending time with the child, or children, I should say. I mean, the girl came up sometimes to stay with us, but not as much as you would think."

"Hmm," Desirae said. "Okay, thanks for tellin' me."

"Did you even know that he had a daughter?" Shawna asked. She now wanted to know a little more about what Tron had told her while she was in a relationship with him. "I mean, did he ever even bring her up to you since the two of you were just fuckin' around on the side?"

Desirae paused for a second while she thought of what she was going to say. "Yes and no," she answered. "I mean, Tron kept so many lies going, as you very well know at this point. I don't even know what to believe out of his mouth anymore. At first, he told me that he owned a restaurant. Next thing you know, I'm seein' his ass on the television, on the news and shit because something done went down at the strip club where he the fuckin' owner. I think I prolly told you some of this after we got in our little thing."

"Yeah, you did a little," Shawna said. "But, I mean, did you know that he had a daughter?"

Desirae nodded. "Yeah," she said. "He mentioned it. But with how his ass is treatin' me right now, I don't know how this is going to work out for me."

Shawna nodded, not saying anything. After all, she really did not have much to say. While she sympathized, in a way, with Desirae because she was another young black woman just like her, she could only feel so much for her because she was fucking around with a man that she knew did not belong to her. Shawna looked at Desirae's stomach, knowing that she was now going to pay the price for being the side chick.

Desirae popped her trunk and began to load the things she'd gotten into her car. It was not really all that cold outside, but every so often the wind would blow a little too hard for her.

"Well, I betta go on," Desirae said. "I'm in the process of movin' and got a lotta shit that I gotta do between now and Friday. I'm sure you know how that is."

"Okay," Shawna said, knowing that the next time she probably saw Desirae , she would probably be almost as big as a house or she would have two little kids following behind her. "Tron ain't no good," she added, trying to comfort Desirae in a strange way. "Don't think that you the only one that he out there doin' wrong. I was with him for years, and we even lived together. And just think about how he kept a lie up and going for so long, to both of us."

Desirae looked back at Shawna. Little snowflakes blew across her face. "Yeah," she said, her words full of regret. "That's one way to look at it. Now, though, he tellin' me that he don't know if I'm even pregnant by him and that I did this shit on purpose and that I was just somethin' to fuck and, you know."

Shawna looked at Desirae, knowing that she was looking at what could have only been described as *hoe in distress*. She felt sorry for her in one way, but could not feel for her in another. The two said goodbye, and Shawna walked to her car.

Desirae finished putting her things into her trunk then hurried to get into the car. Once she started her car, she took a moment to think. "This city is so damn small," she said to herself as she thought about the fact that she'd run into Tron's woman.

As Desirae drove back home, she began to feel overwhelmed by her situation. What made this feeling even worse was the fact that Tron seemed to be getting off rather easy from the situation. Desirae tried to not think about it. She tried to not let it get her riled up. However, by the time she got home, she was really in her feelings. How could a man do a chick that looked so good so wrong?

When Desirae got back into her apartment, she knew exactly what she could do that would really get Tron to see her. She thought about how her father had offered to come down to Indianapolis on Friday and help her with moving back into her mother's house. Desirae smiled, as she thought about Tron being surprised to meet her father. "Oh, Daddy," Desirae said, to herself, smirking. She already knew just how her father would act toward Tron if he so much as said a word that was out of line to his daughter. Desirae pulled her phone out of her pocket and texted Tron, asking him what time on Friday he could come over.

***

Tron wound up having to sit down in his chair so he could let Reese do her thing. She sucked his dick like there was no tomorrow. And there was something about her throat – or maybe there was something about getting in it since Reese had been Desirae's best friend – that drove Tron crazy. He was even able to cum in her mouth and watch her swallow it, with him having to pull her head up off of his dick once it had gotten to the point where it was too sensitive.

Tron traded phone numbers with Reese before she left and went on wherever she was going. He was really feeling himself, liking that Reese gave him less mouth and bitchiness than Desirae did. Reese actually seemed like a cool chick that would go along with the program and not cause any problem. Now, however, Tron would enjoy having this little secret that Desirae did not know about.

Later on that night, after the club was clearing out and the girls were heading out to their cars or to get picked up by their rides, Tyrese came walking up to Tron.

"Nigga, you foul," he said. The two had not had much time for most of the night to really talk without having to worry about people walking up and needing something. "You one foul ass nigga."

Tron smiled. "What, nigga?" he said. "What you mean I'm one foul ass nigga? What the fuck you talkin' about?"

"Nigga, you know," Tyrese said, smiling. "I walked by this fuckin' office when what's her name was up in here. I ain't blind. You had your baby mama's best friend, in your office, on her knees, suckin' your damn dick, nigga. You foul." Tyrese laughed. "You foul as fuck, my dude. Just foul."

Tron shrugged. "So?" he said. "What the fuck you sayin'? Fuck Desirae. She wasn't nothin' but a hoe, anyway. I swear to God I don't know why she ever thought that I was gon' leave my chick to go be with her ass."

Tyrese could see the look of regret in Tron's eyes. That chick Desirae had really shown her ass to Tron, no pun intended, and fucked with his head. "Man, you really shitty about this, ain't you?" Tyrese asked.

"Fuck that chick," Tron said, talking about Desirae. "I swear to God man, the more I think about it, the angrier I get. I saw her ass text me earlier, but I was busy. Watch out, though. She might come walkin' up in here right now or be waitin' out in the parking lot. All that bitch want is some attention."

"Well," Tyrese said. "She bout to have your attention for next twenty fuckin' years. Man, you betta learn how to control that hoe. Give her whatever the fuck she want so she don't go fuckin' your life up, or really killin' you this time around. You know that her ass will. Have you even talked to her about when the babies come?"

"Hell naw," Tron said. "Not yet. I was thinkin' bout what you said and I wanna know if them kids is even mine first before I go paying a fuckin' dime or liftin' a fuckin' finger. I wanna fuckin' know. And I don't give a fuck what she think about it. And as far as I'm concerned, her girl came up in here and was beggin' for the dick. You saw the look in her eyes when she came walkin' up."

"I know," Tyrese said, smiling. "That is exactly why my ass went on walkin' away. I could already tell what she was really comin' up there for. She foul too, but I woulda fucked around with her, too. Can't even lie. She was kinda cute and shit. Had a little bit of a shape, but nothin' to write home about like Desirae. Now, her ass...whew."

Tron looked up at his boy. "Aight, nigga," he said. "Don't need you fuckin' gettin' into shit with your boy or nothing."

"Man, fuck you," Tyrese said. He walked away then came back with his coat. "You wanna smoke tonight?"

Tron shrugged. "Yeah, maybe," he answered. "But you wanna know what I really feel like doin'?"

"What?" Tyrese asked, wanting to know more. He pulled his phone out of his pocket. "You wanna call some bitches over, bruh? I know these hoes over on the west side that will do..."

"Naw, nigga," Tron said, cutting Tyrese off. "Not exactly. Shit, I need some pussy. And I think I know just who I'mma get it from."

Tyrese looked at Tron, seeing that his facial expression was just a little too mischievous. "Man," Tyrese said. "What the fuck you gon' do? You ain't gon go try to fuck your pregnant bitch, is you? You know that kinda shit is gon' make her ass act even more crazy. Don't do it man, don't do it."

Tron shook his head. "Naw," he said. "I'mma have her girl, Reese, over."

Tyrese shook his head then chuckled. "Damn, nigga," he said. "You one coldhearted motherfucka to do some shit like that."

"Yeah, well," Tron said, thinking of how Desirae had not done him any better. "I ain't with Shawna no more, and I never was with Desirae. If her friend wanna come over and have some of the dick, who the fuck am I to get in the way and stop her from doin' what she wanna do? And just because I can, I'mma dick her down real good. So good that Desirae gon' hear me from the otha side of town."

***

Tron and Tyrese smoked a blunt together when they got back to Tron's townhouse. The two of them talked about this and that, with Tyrese bringing up some girls that were interested in trying to come up to Honeys East and make

91

some money. All the while the two of them talked, Tron was texting Reese. And, just as he thought, she was totally down to come over for the night and "chill" with him.

"So, nigga, where you gon' go?" Tron asked Tyrese.

Tyrese looked at his boy. "What the fuck you mean where I'mma go?"

"You know that chick Reese is comin' over," Tron said. "Nigga, I'm bout to smash that pussy like it was my last. I been over here just thinkin' about Desirae. And I swear, she make me mad."

"Yeah," Tyrese said. "I can see that. Man, where the fuck I'mma go at this time of night on the last minute? It's like fuckin' two o'clock and shit. Man, I can just go ahead and lay down and shit while she here."

"Aight, nigga," Tron said. "Whatever. She gon' be here in like fifteen minutes."

"Damn," Tyrese said, putting his hand over his mouth. "Did that bitch wake up out her sleep to come get the dick or what?"

Tron snickered. "Basically, nigga," he said. "You shoulda seen the way she was lookin' at it when I pulled it out earlier, up at the club. Man, it was her fuckin' dream come true."

"Ha," Tyrese said.

Within ten minutes, Tron's phone was vibrating. It was Reese, texting. She was telling him that she was outside and asking which townhouse. Once Tron had given Reese the house number, a few seconds passed and there was knock at the door. Tron and Tyrese looked at one another, knowing exactly what the other one was thinking. Tron got up and walked over to the front door thinking about how Desirae had really pushed him into doing what he was doing – fucking around with the very chick that used to be her best friend.

Bitch shoulda kept her mouth shut, Tron thought. *She been tellin' her best friend about my dick and now she just got to have some and try it out for herself. When will bitches learn that they just need to be quiet.*

Tron pulled the front door open. His eyes met with Reese's eyes as she stepped into the apartment, clearly a little nervous about being there. She looked at the nice furniture that Tron had in his townhouse. It was laid out so well that Reese instantly felt comfortable by just being there.

"Hey," Reese said, smiling.

Tron pushed the front door closed, behind Reese. "Wassup?" he said. "We gon' be upstairs. My boy is down here in the living room and shit, you know?"

"Okay," Reese said, heading up the steps. "I hope it ain't too late for me to come through."

"Naw," Tron said as he followed Reese up the steps. "You came right on time, okay?"

Reese giggled. "Okay," she said.

Tron guided Reese to his bedroom. Once the two of them were inside, he pushed the door closed.

"Relax," Tron said. "Chill out and shit and sit down on the bed." Tron motioned toward the bed.

Reese smiled and sat down, looking around at the nice furniture in Tron's bedroom. "You have a really nice place," she said.

"Thank you," Tron said. "Wait up, before I get comfortable, do you smoke?"

Reese smirked, thinking about it. "Yeah," she said. "Sure."

"Aight," Tron said. "Hold up."

Tron rushed down the steps and grabbed the blunt that he and Tyrese had been smoking. They had only smoked about half of it, or so. Tyrese was just about to smoke the rest of it when Tron came right on up and snatched it. He snickered. "Yeah, nigga," Tron said. "I'm takin' this shit. I'm bout to beat this pussy up."

Tyrese shook his head. "Nigga, you foul," he said. "You foul."

"Yeah, whatever," Tron said and headed back upstairs.

Once Tron got back up to his bedroom, Reese was looking at him. The look on her face told him that she had probably been waiting on him to get back.

"Aight," Tron said, pushing the door closed. "I'm back."

"Oh, okay," Reese said.

Tron sat next to her on the bed and they passed the blunt back and forth while they talked about this and that. Tron could tell that Reese was nervous. He was glad that she was smoking with him, so she could relax a little.

Eventually, Tron was leaning back on his elbows. Reese couldn't help but look at him. She could tell that he had a nice body underneath the clothing. She had watched the way he walked not only when she went back to his office with him but also when he had walked her upstairs to his bedroom. Everything about Tron screamed swag. And she loved it. She had never messed around with a dude like this, and she felt so lucky to finally be having her turn.

Just as Reese was thinking, she felt Tron rub the back of her head. Her eyes rolled back, loving how strong and masculine his hands felt.

"So, wassup?" Tron said, with sleepy eyes. They had just finished the blunt and Tron was ready to get deep inside of that pussy. "What you come over here for?"

Reese smiled, glancing down at Tron's crotch. "Nothin'," she said, not knowing what else she could say.

"Oh, nothin'?" Tron said then smirked. "So, that dick you was suckin' on earlier was just nothin', huh? Okay. I see how you is." He smiled.

Reese playfully bumped Tron. "Naw, that ain't what I meant," she said. "I mean, you know why I'm here, Tron. You know."

Tron looked at Reese. He could already pick up on the fact that she was just an all around sweeter girl than Desirae was. He continued rubbing her head a little bit. "Well, he said. "Why don't you take it out? Stop teasin' a nigga, damn."

Reese giggled as she finally got to the moment that she'd been waiting on. She leaned over and took Tron's dick out of his pants. Tron smiled as he looked at Reese's reaction. She looked at his dick, yet again, as if she had never seen anything so beautiful and dark. Within seconds, Tron's head was leaning back as he was moaning from feeling her silky mouth. "Suck it," he told her. "Suck that dick."

Just then, Tron decided to take control. He needed to let some stress off – stress that had been caused by Desirae.

He gripped the back of Reese' head and pushed it down, as far as it would go, until she was gagging. He took complete control of her head, while she did little to nothing to resist. Reese slid off of the bed and was on her knees in front of Tron. She sucked his dick as if she had not had anything to eat all day.

"You think you can take this dick?" Tron asked. "You think you can take it without runnin' from it? Damn, girl, you suck dick even better than your friend, well, old friend do. Shit, this shit feel good."

Reese pulled her head off and wiped her forearm across her watery eyes. She smiled, liking that Tron had just told her she was better than Desirae. Desirae was so full of herself that Reese knew that if she heard something like that, she would probably throw another one of her fits. Reese nodded, stroking her hand up and down Tron's wet shaft. "Yeah," she said. "I can take it. I wanna take it."

"You on the pill or shot or whatever?" Tron asked. "I can't be havin' no more fuckin' fuck ups like your stupid ass friend. I told her that I can't really be wearin' condoms and shit. They too fuckin' tight on this dick for me. Plus, the shit is always breakin'."

"I bet," Reese said. She stood up and pulled her pants down to the floor. She slid out of her shoes and pants then slid her shirt up over her head. All the while she got naked, she was feeling a kind of excitement that she had never felt before. Tron's dick looked so good. "And yeah," Reese said, finally answering Tron's question about whether or not she was on birth control. "I'm on the shot. And stay up on it, just so you know."

"Bet," Tron said. Tron then leaned forward and kissed Reese's slender, naked torso. Once she was fully undressed, he turned her around and looked at her ass. He slapped it, causing her to giggle a little. Once Tron got a good look at her body, he leaned back on the bed and motioned for Reese to sit on his dick. And Reese did just that.

As Reese lowered herself down, she could not help but to grip her stomach. It was so damn good, and she was feeling stretched like she had never felt before. After a few minutes, once she was accustomed to Tron's size, the two of them were in the full swing of things. Once Reese got done riding him, Tron had flipped her over and was giving her the best long strokes of her life. He gripped her waist as she screamed and squealed, telling him how good he felt and about the orgasms that she was having. Tron literally put his back into fucking Reese, knowing that if Desirae knew, it would literally drive her crazy.

Tron leaned over and whispered in Reese's ear, knowing that he had completely mind-fucked her at this point. "Damn, your pussy is good as fuck, girl," he told her, complementing her. "Betta than Desirae's. Fuck!"

Chapter 7

Last night had been another one of those nights where the loneliness that Desirae felt was enough to practically drive her crazy. While she cleaned up her apartment and got her entire packing process started, there was just no way around her thinking about Tron. What made matters worse was the fact that she, yet again, had sent him a text message about Friday. And, as usual, he did not respond to her. The more and more she thought about it, the more and more she liked the idea of Tron just so happening to meet her father. There were moments when she could only snicker to herself at the very thought of how George would react to meeting Tron, and vice versa.

Desirae packed some of the lighter, less important things into her car to take to her mother's house. However, Desirae decided that since Tron wanted to play game – play ghost, really –, she would go ahead and take the long way to her mother's house. She just so happened to take the way that would bring her right by Tron's place. Just like she had done yesterday, she casually pulled into the parking lot and made her way across until she was outside of Tron's townhouse. She slowed down and looked, seeing that his car was indeed parked out front.

"Well," Desirae said to herself. "Good to see that the nigga is at least still alive and shit."

Desirae decided that she was going to be a better person. She was not going to walk up to his door and talk to him, just yet. Instead, she was going to wait and play her cards right. She wanted to play real nice and get back on his good side so that he would come over on Friday and help her move – and meet her father. She was just not going to put up with how he had been talking to her.

When Desirae circled around the parking lot, she noticed something that she had not seen the first time. A car that looked too familiar was parked outside of Tron's townhouse. Instead of sitting out in the parking lot and burning up her gas, Desirae went ahead and pulled into a parking spot nearby. She wanted to see if this car belonged to who she thought it belonged to. And Desirae knew just how she was going to figure that out. She remembered that, since forever, Reese had this old air freshener hanging in her windshield on the rearview mirror. It was one of the tree ones that were so common, but Desirae remembered a few times when she had seen Reese writing some things on it.

Desirae marched her ass over to the car that she just knew had to belong to Reese. As she walked, she looked up at Tron's townhouse and just imagined what was going on in there. Could Reese be that fucking low and find a way to get at Tron and now spent the night at his place? Was she the reason that Tron had gotten so much quieter – a lot slower at responding to Desirae's text messages?

Desirae walked up on the car. Yep! It was the same color and the same model. She did not ride with Reese all that often, but this car, just by looking at it, had Reese written all over it. Desirae then walked up to the driver's window. She held her hands at the side of her face and looked into the window.

"Fuckin' bitch," Desirae said. "This fuckin' bitch." She stepped back and kicked the bottom of Reese's car. Desirae looked up at where she knew Tron's bedroom was. She felt so damn disgusted that she could not help but shake her head. Never in her entire life had she seen a bitch that was as thirsty and desperate as Reese. This was truly something that Desirae never in a million years thought that she would see. Her stomach hurt in a million fucking ways.

"I don't fuckin' believe this," Desirae said. She kicked Reese's car over and over again. She didn't stop until she had exhauster herself.

For a moment, Desirae contemplated going up to the door and knocking just to see if that nigga Tron would even answer the door. But she decided that this approach just was not going to work out how she would want because she was liable to really kill a nigga, and an ex friend, at this moment. The very thought of Reese fucking around with Tron, behind her back even though they weren't friends any more, was enough to make Desirae really want to kill the both of them. She would not even give two fucks if they were naked and in bed upstairs – if she had to use both of her hands and feet to strangle Tron then Reese's old simple ass – it would be well worth it.

Desire climbed into her car and leaned back, looking out at the snowy parking lot. She wanted to cry. But she knew that neither one of them niggas would be worth her tears at this point.

"I trusted her," Desirae said to herself. "I fuckin' trusted her. That was my fuckin' friend. First, I caught her ass try'na get at Tron up in the fuckin' club, with that dumb ass look on her face. Next thing I know, that bitch is over here and fuckin' him too." Desirae's mother's words of advice about trust, which she had so eloquently given her daughter on numerous occasions throughout her childhood, came flooding back into Desirae's mind. She just never thought that Reese would be the one to do this. After all, Reese was the one who was always so supportive of Desirae's love life, or so she thought. *Reese was always there for me whenever I needed her*, Desirae thought.

With flared nostrils and rage brewing deep in the depths of Desirae's heart, she pulled out of the parking lot. For some reason, she was strangely happy that there was snow and ice on the ground. If there had not been, then Desirae would have probably rammed her car into Reese's car over and over and over again. So bad, Desirae wanted to get out of her car and just go fuck up Reese's car as if somebody was paying her per ounce of destruction.

"Nope," Desirae said, to herself. "I'm done bein' this fuckin' nice. This shit don't make no damn sense."

Desirae knew just what she was going to do. And tomorrow night would be the perfect time to get the ball rolling, so to speak.

***

When Desirae saw Tron's number pop up on her phone later that day, she almost wanted to laugh. It was getting to the point where his lies – his stories, if you will – were just so damn entertaining. She had gone to her mother's house, where she unloaded some of her stuff and calmed down. Now, she was thinking so much more clearly than she had been thinking.

"Let me see what the fuck is gon' come outta this nigga's mouth today," Desirae said, as she picked the phone up and answered. "Hello?"

"I see you called me," Tron said. "You called me yesterday and shit?"

"Yeah, I did," Desirae said. She put on her nicest voice – so nice that Sesame Street characters would have a hard time being nicer than she was being right then. "I was just callin' to see if you could really help me move and shit tomorrow." She smiled. "I ain't found nobody who can come help me, and since you said that you would do it, I thought I would ask you. I don't wanna hurt myself or nothin'."

"Yeah," Tron said, sounding very calm – sounding as if he himself was smiling on the other end.

Desirae smirked and rolled her eyes. Now more than anything she wanted to ask if this nigga was laying up with Reese. However, that was all irrelevant at this point to Desirae. She was going to make sure that Tron got exactly what he had coming to him. *If he thinks getting stabbed with a fork was something...*, Reese thought as she shook her head.

"What time you need me to come over and help?" Tron asked.

"Oh, I don't know," Desirae answered. "You ain't gotta come real early or nothin'," she said. "Why don't you just be here by like eleven or something? How is that?"

"You got a truck and shit?" Tron asked. "How you plannin' on movin' your shit to your mama's house? You got a truck or naw?"

"No, not yet," Desirae told him. "I was going to call this place down Thompson later on and see if they had a truck. I drove by there not too long ago, like a couple days ago, and I saw that they had some sort of special going. And they had plenty of vans and trucks and shit parked out in that lot, so I figured that I could go on over there and get something or whatever."

"Bet," Tron said. "Look here, I can help you out on that too. Let me make some calls and see what I can get and shit.

100

You ain't gotta worry, okay. I'mma get that truck for you. And I'll be there tomorrow, around eleven or whenever."

Well, well, well, Desirae thought. It definitely sounded as if Tron had a bit of a pep in his step, so to speak. He was being kind of nice – nicer than he would normally be to her, especially nowadays.

"Okay," Desirae said. "That works."

The two of them hung up. Desirae then scrolled through her recent calls. She got to her father and called him.

"Yeah, hello?" George answered.

"Hey, Daddy," Desirae said. "Did I catch you at a bad time or what?"

"Naw, baby," George said. "You cool, you cool? What's goin' on? You still want me to come down tomorrow and help you move and stuff? Don't think I ain't been thinkin' bout that."

"Actually," Desirae said. She smiled. "Daddy, that is what I was callin' you about – funny you mention it. I wanted to know if you were coming and if you could be here around noon. Don't flip out or nothin', but you will actually get to meet Tron. He will here around that time. And he gettin' a truck on his way over here, so I don't have to worry about that."

"Awe, yeah?" George said. "Okay, okay. I can get up and get down there by then. Don't you worry, baby. I'll be there."

Desirae thanked her father and they talked about this and that for a few minutes. When she hung up with him, she felt so evil. Now? Now, she just needed to think of a way to get Reese back for fucking around with Tron. Sure, she could very well wait until she gave birth. However, that would be a long six months to wait to jump on Reese and beat that ass.

Desirae pondered for some minutes before she got back up and moved around her apartment, continuing to pack. For some reason, she had never felt as happy as she felt right then. There was nothing like watching, and taking part in, someone getting just what they deserve. And nothing could be further from the truth than when that somebody has actually done you wrong. Desirae was determined to think of what she was going to do to get Reese back. And whatever she decided to do, it was going to be worthwhile.

***

When Tron hung up the phone, he looked over at Reese and smiled. She may not have the baddest body like Desirae, but she had a pussy that just would not quit. Tron wound up going for three rounds last night with Reese because it was so damn good. In fact, they did not even sleep until around five o'clock in the morning from all the fucking that they were doing.

Reese, clearly a mess of a woman, woke up just as Tron was on the phone talking to Desirae. When he hung up, she looked at him. A brief wave of guilt came over her, but she could not and would not deny one very true thing: last night, with Tron, was hands down the best dick that she had ever had in her life. She lost count of how many times she orgasmed. It was just amazing.

"Was that Desirae?" Reese asked just as Tron was setting the phone back down.

Tron nodded. "Yeah," he said. "I'm supposed to be helpin' her move back to her mama's house tomorrow."

"Oh, yeah?" Reese said. "You don't think that she thought I was here or nothing, do you?"

Tron shook his head. "Naw," he said. "You ain't say nothin' when I was on the phone with her. She ain't even ask me where I was or nothin'. I just wanted to make sure that I called her back before her ass is over here actin' crazy, or worse, up at the club tonight or somethin'. I ain't got no more time for her games and bullshit. I'm just try'na be coo until they babies drop and shit."

"So, she is havin' twins? You sure of that?" Reese asked.

Tron shrugged. "Fuck if I know," he said. "I mean, that is what she told me, and I don't know why a chick would lie about some shit like that. But, the more and more I think about it, she prolly out in these streets and fuckin' a lotta niggas, don't she?"

Reese looked away while she thought. "I guess," she answered. "Everywhere we would go, niggas would be hollerin' at her."

"Yeah," Tron said. "I bet." He imagined her body. And it amazed him how a woman with such a beautiful body could be so damn bitchy and selfish at the core. "She not like you. She a hoe."

Reese playfully tapped Tron's toned chest. "Don't say that," she said. "She used to be my friend."

"Y'all ain't friends no more, are you?" Tron asked, already knowing the answer.

Reese let out a sigh. "Naw," she said, trying to think of how to explain her point of view. "Desirae...Desirae... It's like she think that she's better than me or something. All she ever talked about was herself and her body and anything else to do with her. Then, she had the nerve to basically call me ugly and shit, prolly just cause I'm not build like she is."

Tron liked how Reese was opening up to him. Sure, she was just a fuck as well, but the fact that she was telling him exactly what he wanted to know about Desirae was more than enough. He was just looking for the right reasons to demand that Desirae go through with a paternity test. The more and more Reese talked about Desirae's provocative habits and clothes that she wore out in the street, the clearer it was becoming to him that he needed to make sure that hoe was pregnant by him and not some other nigga. Bitches were always looking for a way to come up on a nigga's success. And Tron was not going to let that kind of shit happen with him.

Tron lay up in the bed with Reese for a little while longer. He contemplated dicking her down one good time before they left, but decided against it. He had things to do and really didn't have time. There would be a next time because she had the kind of pussy that he could really get used to having on a regular basis.

Tron walked Reese downstairs and to the front door. Reese, looking like she had stars in her eyes from last night, turned around before she walked out the door and said that she would text him. Tron nodded and said he would do the same, as he pushed the front door closed. No sooner than he could turn all the way around, Tyrese was there. His boy was walking right toward him, with a grin on his face.

"Damn, nigga," Tyrese said. "You was upstairs Mandingo-in that bitch last night."

Tron shrugged. "Had to," he said, in a very matter of a fact way. "I was up there long dickin' that pussy. A fuckin' grudge fuck is what you call that."

"I knew it, I knew it," Tyrese said, his balled up fist up over his mouth. "I knew that was exactly what yo ass was doin', nigga. Fuckin' her to get back at your baby mama. Man...she gon' kill you when she find out."

"Man, whatever," Tron said. He walked right on passed Tyrese and made his way to the kitchen. Tyrese followed behind Tron as he continued. "She prolly ain't gon find out," he said. "And if she do, I could give two fucks less about that hoe. Fuck that bitch. If she wasn't pregnant, supposedly, with my kids and shit, I prolly wouldn't ever even talk to her again and shit. Just ignore that bitch like the piece of trash that she is."

"So now you done spent the night, long dickin' her old best friend," Tyrese said. "Man, I'm tellin' you, once she find that shit out, she is gonna make your life a fuckin' hell. Mark my words, nigga. She will, most definitely, find out about that. You know how chicks be and shit. If the Reese chick is mad at her old friend, she gon say something to Desirae eventually that she thinks Desirae don't know about – the one leg up, kind of thing, I guess. You know how chicks be, nigga. You already know. Don't be brand new with me, bruh."

"Fuck all that," Tron said. "And they not even friends no more, or that's what Reese was sayin' when we was layin' up in the sheets and shit. So, really, if you think about it, I ain't do shit wrong. As far as Desirae know, I met that bitch somewhere and ain't even know who she was or that she was her old best friend. Ain't like Desirae ever introduced us or nothin', no way. Fuck her and whatever she think. I know that bitch tried to trap me. Some of the shit Reese was tellin' me about that hoe."

"Is it bad?" Tyrese asked. "Like, did she have that kinda pussy that just about every nigga in the city done ran through and shit."

Tron looked at his boy, not wanting to admit what he was about to admit. He nodded "Yeah, I guess," he said. "I mean, she definitely wasn't no pure, virgin kinda bitch or nothin'. That's for sure."

"Man, I told you what you betta do," Tyrese said. "I told you that yo ass better get a fuckin' DNA test or whatever they call it so you can make sure that she ain't just try'na get paid off of your ass. You know these games that these hoes out here, especially nowadays, will play on a nigga. Man, trust me bruh. You betta get that shit just so that yo ass can be sure."

Tron pulled a gallon of orange juice out of the refrigerator and set it on the kitchen counter. He nodded his head. "Yeah, that's what I'mma do," he told his boy Tyrese. "I'mma be over there tomorrow, helpin' her move back in with her mama and shit."

"Look at your ass," Tyrese said, holding back a big snicker. "She already got your ass on daddy patrol. Watch her crazy ass be pullin' out the phone tomorrow when you get over there and try to take pictures and shit so she can put'em up on her Instagram or some shit."

Tron looked at his boy Tyrese. "Nigga, fuck you," he said. "I ain't bein' in no picture with that hoe."

Tyrese walked away. "I got shit I gotta do today," he said. "I'm tellin' you, nigga. Watch your back. Once that chick find out that you fucked her old best friend, she probably gon' drop a fuckin' bomb on you or some shit. She already tried to kill your ass – cause of death: stabbed to death by a fork. All she need now is a real good reason to really go psycho bitch on your ass.

Tron shook his head. "Yeah," he said. "Same goes to you. Watch out for Nalique, before she come beat that ass and shit and have you runnin' back over here cryin', again."

"Yeah, yeah, whatever," Tyrese said. "Whatever."

Chapter 8

When Desirae finished packing up some more of her stuff, all that was left in its original place in her apartment was the television, the entertainment system, and her bed. Everything else was packed into boxes or stuffed into bags. She knew that she was going to get hungry soon, so she thought she would go out to grab something to eat rather than taking the time, and energy, to cook something. Just then, as she decided that, she also decided that tonight just might be the night to go see Reese.

"She was callin' me, beggin' for forgiveness," Desirae said. "And I'mma give it to her."

Desirae grabbed her phone and went right to Reese's number. She called, looking forward to hear what front she put on when they both damn well knew that she had been laying up with Tron in the middle of the day. Why else would she ever, ever, ever be over at Tron's house? Why else would she have been in that bar, ducked off to the side? Desirae knew that she needed to be as nice as she could be so that Reese would not think anything was up.

"Hello?" Reese answered.

Desirae laughed. Reese sounded as if she was clearly surprised at the fact that she was calling her. "Hey, Reese," she said. "It's Desirae."

"Oh…" Reese said. "Hey?"

"Oh, I'm sorry, girl," Desirae said. "I ain't catch you at no bad time or nothin', did I?"

Before Desirae could even come to the finish line of her sentence, Reese was already answering. "Naw, naw," she said. "You ain't catch me at a bad time."

"Okay," Desirae said. "Well, I was thinkin' about the other day and stuff. And I still don't know if I trust you to be my friend and shit, Reese. I just thought I would call you because I'mma be goin' out and gettin' somethin' to eat in a minute and was thinkin' maybe I could stop by and we chat for a minute or somethin'?"

"Well," Reese said, clearly sounding hesitant. "I guess that would be okay. You don't wanna talk over the phone, girl? You was pretty mad at me, from what it sounded like."

"Exactly," Desirae said. "I'm not about to let no nigga come between me and my best friend. You said you was up there to just see what that nigga was up to so that you could come back and tell me. I thought more and more about that and thought about how crazy I musta been, trying to accuse you of try'na do something with the father of my unborn children."

"Yeah," Reese said. "I told you that we hadn't done anything."

Desirae looked down at her phone and shook her head. "Yeah," she said. "I know."

Desirae was disgusted beyond words.

"Okay, well," Reese said. "When was you try'na come through, girl?"

Desirae checked the time on her phone. "Shit," she said. "What you doin' right now? I can come right now, if that would be cool with you. You know what the roads are like out there today? I haven't been out much lately, so..."

"The roads?" Reese said. "They good, Desirae. You know how some of the side streets be. They be kinda bad – messed up. But the main streets are clear, girl. You'll be alright."

"Okay," Desirae said, very calmly. "Well, I'm about to get some clothes on and head over that way."

"Okay," Reese said. "Girl, let me know when you close."

On that note, the two said bye and Desirae dropped her phone onto her couch.

"I'mma fuck that bitch up so bad," Desirae said to herself, talking about Reese. She could feel her blood pumping. It was hard to not walk around her apartment with balled fists. As Desirae got dressed, she was so happy that she did absolutely nothing to Reese's car when she was parked outside of Tron's place. The element of surprise was one of the oldest tricks in the book. And Desirae was getting a thrill from using it herself. Reese would never know what was coming. And, if everything went according to how Desirae wanted, Tron would never know either. She was already thinking of how she could get Tron to show his real colors tomorrow. All she needed was to get him going, at the right time. She hoped that God would be on her side for this one.

Chapter 9

It took Desirae twenty minutes to get over to Reese's neighborhood. Since Reese stayed with her family, and her family had always been so nice to Desirae, she had decided while she was driving that she would at least be respectful enough to not beat the bitch's ass in front of her home – in front of her family. Plus, Desirae knew that if she did that, her family would be the ones trying to come out and save a hoe. And Desirae did not want for anybody to get in the way, not for one second.

When Desirae pulled up outside of Reese's house, which was in the hood, she called Reese and told her that she was outside waiting. Rather than her coming inside, Desirae suggested that they go somewhere to eat together. Just as Desirae hoped and planned, Reese agreed. Within minutes, she came rushing out of the front door, down the steps, and across the front yard. When Reese got into Desirae's car and closed the door, she looked at Desirae. The look in her eyes said it all: she felt guilty about something. Desirae got a kick out of the fact that she knew what Reese thought she did not know.

"Hey," Reese said. Something about this was just not feeling right to her.

"Hey," Desirae said. She then forced a smile. "I was thinkin' we go eat together somewhere. What is over here?"

Reese explained the number and types of fast food restaurants that lined a nearby busy road. Desirae pulled off, after saying that going to that particular street was just fine. She drove toward the corner in silence. Soon enough, the silence was too much – like a train coming – for Reese. She just had to say something – anything – to break the ice.

"Desirae, girl," Reese said. "I swear to God I was just up in there try'na see what he was doin'."

Desirae looked over at Reese. "I know, I know," she said, nodding her head just as she turned the corner. "The more I thought about it, the more I knew. That's why I finally called you."

"Okay," Reese said. "I just hate that you thought that I would do something like that to you. Girl, how long have we known each other? I would never do nothing like that to you."

Desirae pulled up at a stoplight – a stoplight that was situated at a corner that was rather dead during the night, especially during the winter months. She looked across at Reese and shook her head. "Girl, you is a damn lie."

Immediately, Reese could feel her heart start to pound in her chest. Something just seemed a little too nice about Desirae, especially with the fact that she called after ignoring Reese for the better part of two weeks. "What are you talkin' bout, Desirae?" Reese asked. "What you mean I'mma damn lie?"

Quickly, Desirae threw her car into PARK and began to take her seatbelt off. When she was finished, she looked her former best friend dead in the eye. "I mean just what the fuck I said!" she yelled. "How the fuck you gon' get in my car and just tell a bold face lie, to my face like that, like I don't fuckin' know. I know just what you was doin' up in that club that night. And you know it too, so I don't even know why you try'na lie. You just a thirsty ass bitch because you couldn't get no good dick on your own."

"See, Desirae," Reese said, getting a little mad herself. "I don't know where you get all this attitude and shit from, I swear."

"You don't?" Desirae asked. "You don't? Is that what you really gon' say? Girl, I see you for what you really is. No sooner than I really started to think that maybe you was up in that club that night for whatever reason you came up with just now and said, what the fuck happens, huh? Tell me why I rolled by Tron's place earlier and saw your car there? Huh, tell me that!"

Reese backed up, like an animal trapped in a corner. How did Desirae just so happen to know that she was over at Tron's place? She was there when Tron was on the phone with Desirae, and she was sure that he did not say a word about her being there. Quickly, she knew that she needed to say something that would make sense for saying that it was not her. Reese shook her head. "No, Desirae," she said. "No, I swear. I wasn't over there today or whenever. That wasn't my car."

Just then, Desirae reached out as quickly as she could and slapped the shit out of Reese. A light scream spilled over Reese's lips as she gripped her face. The sides had already been stinging from being out in the cold weather. Getting slapped in the face was just incredibly painful.

"Bitch, I know that was your fuckin' car!" Desirae let Reese know. "I looked inside and saw that same ole raggedy ass air freshener that you done had since for fucking ever. Look at you, lyin' and shit to my fuckin' face again."

A tear rolled down Reese's face. "Well, damn, Desirae," she said. "You ain't have to slap me."

Desirae snickered, looking at how weak of a woman Reese truly was. She was going to enjoy beating that ass, even if it was the last thing in the world that she ever did.

"Didn't have to slap you?" Desirae asked. "Girl, I'm bout to give you way worse than that."

No sooner than Reese could process what was being said, she felt Desirae grab a fistful of her hair and pull her face down and into the driver's seat. Desirae pushed her car door open as she stepped.

"Stupid bitch!" Desirae yelled, tightening her grip on Reese's hair. "I swear to God, bitch. I'mma beat that ass so bad."

Reese squirmed, flailing her arms about. However, with Desirae standing outside of the car, Reese could not reach her while being held over the consul like a rag doll. Not letting her grip up one bit, Desirae held Reese's head down with one hand and began to punch the sides with the other. She hit Reese in the head over and over and over again. She didn'tstop until she was too tired to keep her grip on Reese's hair. When she fell back and into the street on her side of the car, there was a clump of Reese's hair entangled in Desirae's hand.

"Bitch, you was my fuckin' best friend," Desirae said, now in deep in her emotions. "And you gon go behind my back and fuck Tron and shit. All the shit I was tellin' you all these weeks and months and you was really just savin' that shit so you could get you some too."

Reese pushed her car door open and climbed out, into the snow along the curb.

"Bitch, why the fuck you think that a man like that is gon' want some hoe like you?" Reese snapped back. "Girl, all you ever talked about was yourself. You know niggas just want you to have somethin' to fuck. They would never take your hoe ass home to they family or not shit."

"Oh, yeah?" Desirae said, heading around the front of the car to get Reese. "You ain't gon' call me no hoe but you the one laid up with him over there, behind my fuckin' back."

Reese stepped back at Desirae got close to her, but her movement was too late. Before she knew it, Desirae was swinging at her head like there was no tomorrow. Reese swung back, like any grown woman would, but Desirae's swings were too fast. Her licks were too hard. And, more importantly, it was so damn cold outside.

"Now, what, bitch?" Desirae said. "Huh? Now what? You gettin' that ass beat, bitch! You gettin' that ass beat!"

A car rolled by, swerving around Desirae's parked car at the stoplight. Desirae knew that she needed to hurry up and get her point across. The last thing she needed was some nigga deciding to be a good citizen by calling the police on her. What she was doing was completely justified, at least in her mind. Within a matter of seconds, Reese was down on the ground, in the snow. And Desirae was not letting her up. She did not give two fucks about the red dots that were popping up here and there in the snow. For all she cared, Reese could leak until she fucking died out there in the cold.

Reese swung back, but couldn't make contact. Desirae laughed at her as she grabbed another handful of Reese's hair with one hand. She used her other hand to really give it to Reese, punching her in her face until her hand hurt. After a good long while, Desirae stood up and looked around. She then looked down at Reese, who was struggling to get back up on her feet, and saw that her phone had fallen out of her pocket. She could see the end of it sticking out of the snow.

Quickly, knowing that this was just what she wanted, Desirae reached down and picked it up.

"I swear to God," Desirae said. "I don't ever wanna see your ugly, no body havin' ass again in life. I fuckin' hate you, bitch. I fuckin' hate you."

Reese wiped the blood away from her face as she watched Desirae walk back around the front of her car and get back inside. All while she walked to her side of the car, eye contact was never broken. Within seconds, Reese realized what Desirae pulling off and leaving her outside in the middle of a winter night would mean. Quickly, she stumbled back over to the curb and reached at the car door handle. Just as she did, she heard the car locks go down in one big thump. Desirae pulled off.

"Fuck you, bitch!" Reese yelled, as Desirae's car got further and further away. "Fuck you ,bitch! He said he liked my shit more than yours anyway."

Reese, frustrated at having suffered at the rage of Desirae out on the sidewalk, brushed the clumpy snow off of her coat and turned around. She headed home, alternating between grabbing each side of her face. They stung so bad as she walked the five or six blocks in the snow to get back home. Just as she got a good block away from the corner where Desirae had forced her out of the car, she noticed that she did not her phone on her. Immediately, she looked back, not even knowing where to begin looking to see if she could find where she had dropped it.

***

"Yes!" Desirae yelled as she drove away from Reese. "Yes! I beat that bitch's ass like it was nothin'."

Desirae was in such a celebratory mood that she went ahead and headed to the nearest White Castles. She had told herself that she was going to watch what she ate so that she would not have as much weight to lose after giving birth to the babies. However, when she thought about all of the calories she had just burned beating Reese's ass, she told herself that it would be perfectly okay to have something that she really wanted to eat.

As Desirae got some food and headed home, she prided herself in how slick she was. She could remember, very clearly, the look on Reese's face just before she grabbed that hair and started to get in that ass. To say the least, it was priceless – just priceless. Desirae pulled up outside of her apartment building and headed inside, daring Reese to get in her car tonight and head over to her place. If Reese was stupid enough to do that, then she would be stupid enough to need another ass whooping. However, if she got in that ass out in the parking lot, she would be liable to go on for longer than she did at the corner. That was some bold, brave shit that Desirae did. And she would never forget it either

When Desirae was walking through the front door of her apartment, she could not for the life of her wipe the smile away from her face. It was practically cemented into her face at this point. Just the thought that Reese had gotten exactly what she deserved – exactly what she had coming to her— thrilled Desirae to the core. She headed to her dining room table, pulled a chair out, and sat down to eat her food. When she finished, she pulled Reese's phone out of her pocket. Her plan had been to get Reese's phone so that she would not be able to call Tron and tell him what had happened until – if ever – after Tron had met her father tomorrow. Desirae just didn't think that it would have been so damn easy.

"That shit just fell right out of her pocket," Desirae said, aloud. "I beat that ass. Fuckin' lyin' ass bitch. That's what she get, too. Oh, that look on her face. That shit was fuckin' priceless."

Desirae opened her living room window, which looked down over quite a few things – houses, wooded area, and a little bit of the parking lot. She smiled as she shook her head and hurled Reese's phone into the distance. Before it could even land, wherever it landed, Desirae had already shut the window and was headed back over to the couch. Now, she just had to think about tomorrow. She thought about how in just a little more than twelve hours, Tron would be over here to help her move. It was now up to Desirae to figure out just what she would say to Tron to get him going, and what kind of things she would need to say to get him to react in a way that would make her father jump out of his usual coolness. Desirae felt so evil, but so good at the same time. All of this betrayal was just too much for her. If she was going to be hurting, so were the people who had done her wrong – so were Tron and Reese.

Chapter 10

Tron woke up Friday morning in a bad mood. Last night, the club had been pretty busy, which was good. However, the last thing he wanted to do first thing when he got up was get ready to go help Desirae move to her mama's house. The more he thought about it, the more he was determined to get a paternity test done. Sure, he would go ahead and help her move out of her apartment and into her mama's house. However, he was going to find a way to bring up a paternity test, whether Desirae liked it or not.

Tron slid out of bed, resisting the urge to do a wake and bake. He kind of felt like he would need it, especially since he already knew that Desirae was surely going to start something. He accepted that and went on with his morning, taking a shower then sliding into some old jeans and a long-sleeved white shirt. When Tron was ready, he headed downstairs. Just as he was walking into the kitchen, he could hear Tyrese. He was waking up, on the couch, and already getting to making wisecracks.

"You gon' die today, nigga," Tyrese said. "Somebody gon' die today."

"Nigga, fuck you," Tron said. "I told your ass that shit ain't on' happen. She don't even know that me and Reese fucked around."

"Man, it's been like what?" Tyrese asked. "Like two days or some shit? You really think that Desirae ain't heard that you fucked her old best friend. Trust me, nigga. She know. She know, she know, she know. I don't even know why you settin' yourself up."

"Nigga, you always try'na give relationship advice when you don't even have a relationship to give advice from," Tron said.

"Yeah, well," Tyrese said, getting up off of the couch. "I also ain't been on the news for gettin' stabbed with no fork. But I ain't gon' say nothin' bout that. You know how sensitive your ass get when a nigga keep it real with you."

"Yeah, yeah," Tron said.

"Yeah, yeah, my ass," Tyrese said. "Just watch your ass when you go over there. And make sure that she don't slip nothin' in your drink."

"Nigga," Tron said. "I'mma just go over there and help her move. That's all."

"Ha!" Tyrese said, his voice fading away as he was headed to the bathroom. "That's what you think."

Once Tron got himself some orange juice and ate a couple of cereal bars, he slid into his coat and headed out the door. As he walked down to his car, he wondered why he had not heard from Reese. He was not falling in love with her or anything like that. And, now, he felt like he was probably just feeling a little paranoid from some of the stuff that Tyrese had been saying to him. He shook it all off, saying that Reese would probably text him later on today or something, as he got into his car and pulled off. Last night, when he had a moment to himself at the club, he had gone to the back and arranged to pick up a moving truck for today. All he wanted to do was make sure that everything went as smoothly as possible. No fighting, no arguing. He did not even want to meet her mother. He just wanted to help her carry her stuff so she would not be over there crying about him neglecting her or anything.

Tron rolled over to the moving company not too far from his townhouse and picked up the truck that he had reserved last night. Once he paid and hopped in, he felt a little weird driving something so big, but he managed. He pulled his phone out of his pocket and called Desirae, to let her know that he was on his way.

"Hello?" Desirae answered.

"Hey, wassup," Tron said. "It's me. I was just callin' to tell you that I got the truck and am on my way with it right now. Is your shit packed already or do I gotta help you with that too?"

Desirae took a moment to think, as she looked around her apartment. "Mostly everything is packed," she told him. "I just didn't take down the entertainment system or move the bed cause they both too heavy for me."

"Okay, I'll be over there in a minute," Tron said. He then hung up, without even saying goodbye or anything.

117

***

Desirae snickered to herself as she put her phone back down onto the kitchen countertop. She found it so hilarious how Tron could not even respect her enough to say bye to her when they hung up the phone. He just hung up on her, as if she was nothing and not even worth his time. She could also hear it in his voice. There was no doubt in Desirae's mind that Tron was not all that thrilled about coming over to help her move.

Desirae then remembered that she needed to call her father and see where he was. How close to Indianapolis was he? Desirae did not want him to show up way after she and Tron had moved her stuff. She grabbed her phone and called her father.

"Daddy?" Desirae said when her father answered his phone. "Where you at, Daddy? Are you close?"

"Uh," George said. Desirae figured that her father was probably looking around. "Yeah, I'm close, baby. I think I'll be coming into the city in like fifteen minutes. Then, I'mma be over to you. You still over on the south side, right?"

"Yeah," Desirae said, smiling. "Still the same place."

"Okay, baby," George said. "Well, let me get off this phone. It's startin' to snow a little bit out here. I'll be over there in a minute, I'll be there in a minute."

"Okay, Daddy," Desirae said. The two hung up after saying bye to one another quickly.

Desirae leaned back on the counter. She had practically woken up feeling high. Over and over, she played the scene at the corner last night over in her mind. It was priceless – just too damn priceless. Ever since giving it to Tron's chick Shawna, right there in front of her register at Clarkes up at Lafayette Square, Desirae had definitely felt like she had a little bit more of a fight inside of her. Last night, however, she told herself would be the last time she would use her hands. Today, though, she would use her words – words that she knew would cause Tron to get riled up and really show what kind of a nigga he was. She wanted to see him say some of the things he said to her the other day and just a couple of weeks ago. Telling her that she was just something to fuck was something that Tron just should not have said.

***

When Tron pulled up in front of Desirae's apartment, he could feel a difference in his presence. And no, the difference he was feeling was not just from driving a big moving truck instead of his car. It was from why he was there to begin with. For months, this had been the place he came to when he had a little time away from Shawna to bust a nut. If he knew that Desirae was going to trap him like this, he would have just cut it off after the first time they fucked. He hated himself for falling for a big butt and a nice smile – the oldest trick in the book.

Tron backed the truck up to the building doorway and turned the engine off. Practically dragging his feet, Tron headed inside of the building and up the stairs. Normally, he would just try the door to see if it was open. However, even if it was open, he did not want to send the wrong message to Desirae – he did not want to do anything that would tell her that things were getting back to comfortable between the two of them. On the contrary, for much of the drive down to the south side, Tron was thinking about how and when he was going to tell Desirae that he wanted a paternity test. He just had to know if Desirae was really pregnant by him or not. Some of the things that Reese had said to him the other day really got him thinking. Deep down, Tron wished that Desirae was not pregnant by him. And it wasn't that he wouldn't love the kids if they were his. However, his life would be a hell of a lot easier if Desirae actually had fucked around with some other nigga and gotten pregnant by him.

Tron knocked on the door and waited for Desirae to open it.

"It's open," Desirae announced.

Tron shook his head and knocked again – an action that was letting Desirae know that she actually needed to come to the door and let him inside. Within a few seconds, Desirae yanked the door open. Tron avoided eye contact with her as he stepped inside and looked around.

"I said that the door was open," Desirae said. "Why you ain't just come in?"

"Oh, my bad," Tron said. "I ain't hear you say that. I ain't. I mean, I heard you say somethin' but I didn't know what it was."

"Hmm, hmm," Desirae said. She could smell Tron's shit from a mile away. And he was so full of it that he stunk. "Well," she said, pointing to the packed boxes around the room. "This is my stuff, packed up. You said you got the truck, right?"

Tron nodded, barely opening his mouth to tell her that he did.

"Okay," Desirae said. "I didn't know what to do about the bed and entertainment system, so they the only two things that might be kinda hard to get outta here. I picked the dining room table up a little bit and it ain't so bad. We prolly just gon' have to maneuver it out of the door."

"That's coo," Tron said, nodding. "You got the shit in here, so we can get it back out. Won't be no problem."

On that note, Tron simply began to pick boxes up and carry them out into the hallway then downstairs. Desirae could pick up on how quiet Tron was being – his silence was something that she just could not ignore. Once Tron had made a third trip down to the truck and back, Desirae knew this was the time to get things rolling.

"What's wrong with you, Tron?" Desirae asked. "Ever since you got here, you been givin' me the cold shoulder and shit. It's like you don't even wanna talk to me or nothin', let alone look at me or nothin'."

"I don't," Tron admitted. "Sorry."

Just then, Desirae's neck snapped back. Even though Tron had only said a few words to Desirae since getting to her place, there was something about his tone that was just a little too disrespectful. This was especially so, considering that he had been fucking her former best friend within the last two days. Desirae's top lipped curled up when she thought about it.

"What the fuck is that supposed to mean?" Desirae asked.

"It means just what I said, Desirae," Tron said. "Girl, I ain't come here to argue with your ass or no shit like that, okay? I just came here to help you move this shit so we can get the fuck on with our day."

Before Desirae could even say anything back to Tron's comment, Tron had headed back downstairs with a box. When he returned, he immediately saw that her nostrils were flared up, as if she was really upset about something. Tron looked at her. "What?" he asked in very short tone.

Desirae squinted at Tron. "You really do hate me, don't you?" she asked. "Huh, Tron? Is that what it is? You really do hate me that much, don't you?"

Tron shrugged. "I ain't say that," he said. "So, I don't know why you thinkin' that shit. I ain't say that I hate you or no shit like that at all, Desirae."

"Then tell me this," Desirae said. "Why won't you look me in my eyes, Tron? Tell me that. Why won't you look me in my eyes?"

Tron turned and looked at Desirae. It did not take Desirae long to see the cold look in Tron's eyes. He looked as if he was disgusted with her in every way that he could possibly be. And Desirae did not like that. She was not the one who fucked around even though she belonged to someone, like Tron did. She was not the one who fucked around with the best friend of a chick who was pregnant with his children, that was Tron. Desirae shook her head.

"I swear to God, nigga," Desirae said. "You somethin' else, I swear. First you was talkin' bout bein' with me and leavin' your chick, now I'm just..." Desirae's words trailed off, from her being so angry.

"I want a paternity test," Tron came out and said it. He looked Desirae up and down, not even trying to hide the look of disgust in his face. He had come over here to help her move. And, sure enough, just like he had thought, Desirae was trying to turn all of this into an argument. No matter what he did, this chick just had to go making something out of nothing.

"You want a what, nigga?" Desirae asked, wondering why the fuck something like that would be on his mind at this point.

"Bitch, you heard me," Tron said. His voice was getting a little louder. "I want a fuckin' paternity test."

"Why you even bringin' that shit up again?" Desirae asked. "Huh, Tron? You really just want to believe that these twins that I'm pregnant with ain't yours, don't you? You really is one no good nigga, ain't you, Tron?"

"Bitch," Tron said. "Whatever. I been thinkin' bout this shit for days, and you ain't nothin' but a hoe like I told you. All you wanna do is argue and shit. So, no, if you want the truth, I do not think that I'm the only possible father of whoever, and whatever, you pregnant with."

Desirae looked at Tron, seeing a boy who just had never grown into a man. She could not help but pity him.

"I swear," Desirae said. "This is a-fuckin-mazin' how you actin' now. Just a month ago, you couldn't get enough of this."

"Well, shit done changed since a month ago, Desirae," Tron said. "I don't know what you don't get about that."

"You just mad that I wouldn't be with you no matter what at this point," Desirae said. "Yeah, that's why you mad. You sittin' over there, alone, probably jackin' off and shit because that damn Shawna left your ass. She even saw how no good your ass was. Just another worthless ass nigga, I swear."

Tron shook his head, feeling himself getting to his breaking point. "Be with you?" he asked, talking loudly. "Bitch, you really think I would want to be with someone like you."

Just then, Desirae could hear what sounded like a car pulling up outside. She decided to let Tron go right on with what he was saying, in case it was her father that was pulling up and about to come in.

"And why not?" Desirae asked.

"Why not?" Tron asked, in shock that she would even ask him a question like that. "Why the fuck would a nigga wanna be with you? If it wasn't for your body, and how you suck dick, I woulda never hit you up again after I met you, if you wanna know the truth. Now... Now ain't no tellin' how many niggas done run through that pussy. That's why your ass ain't got no walls now."

122

"Ain't got no walls?" Desirae asked. Now she felt insulted. Never, ever, in her fucking life had she had a man make fun of her insides like that. In fact, if a man ever made any comments about how her insides felt, they were comments that said just how good her pussy was. That, on top of her body and her pretty face, sealed the deal for a lot of niggas. "Nigga, fuck you!" Desirae said, full of rage.

"Naw, bitch," Tron said, now yelling. "Fuck you! All you ever was was a hoe! And, like I said, I want a fuckin' paternity test. Any nigga in his right mind would want one after dealin' with a hoe like you. All you are is a body and nothin' more. Bitch probably can't even do math, ole dumb lookin' bitch."

Just then, Desirae's front door swung open. She looked passed Tron as her father came walking in. The look on his face was the look of mass destruction in every possible way. Desirae knew that her father may have been getting up there in years, but he was still in shape and could go toe to toe with the youngest, and the best, of them any damn day of the week.

Hearing the door open and someone come inside, Tron immediately turned around.

"Who the fuck is old head?" Tron asked, sizing up the man.

"Old head?" George asked. The 5'10" man, who was a little bulky, slowly walked closer and closer to Tron. "Who you callin' old head, young nigga?" he asked. "Better yet," he said. "Tell me who you was callin' a hoe? Who was that I heard you callin' dumb when I came up here?"

"Daddy, don't," Desirae said. She really did not mean for her father to stop, but she knew that she really had to play up being the innocent, young woman.

Tron turned and looked at Desirae. "Daddy?" he said. "You had your fuckin' daddy come over here and didn't even tell me?"

"Why she got to tell you, huh, nigga?" George asked Tron. "Why the fuck she got to tell you for? You don't even live here, or do you?" George looked passed Tron and at his daughter. "Do this nigga, who I'm pretty sure was talkin' to you all disrespectfully and stuff, even live here his damn self?"

Desirae looked at Tron then her father. She shook her head. "No," she said. "Daddy, this is Tron. Remember, I was tellin' you about him?"

George nodded, pushing the front door closed then walking up toward Tron. "Oh, yeah?" he said. "This is the nigga that got you pregnant, huh? This the nigga? And now he up in here callin' my baby girl all types of shit like he done lost his mind or something?"

Even though Tron was at least half of the man's age, he could not help but feel a little intimidated. Not only did he look a little rough around the edges, he also looked like the kind of old cat who had never lost his way when it came to using his fists. Tron backed up, ever so slightly, putting a little distance between Desirae's father and himself.

"Look, that ain't what I meant," Tron said, knowing that he had to at least try to clean up whatever Desirae's father had heard him saying to her. As Tron himself was a father, he knew that there were certain things he did not want to ever hear a man say to his daughter.

"Well, what did you mean, Tron?" George asked. "What did you mean when you called my little girl a hoe? Huh? What did you mean when you was sayin' all that shit to her like that? Come on, young buck. I may be gettin' a little older, but I ain't deaf. I know what I heard you say, and I don't like it. I don't like it at all."

Desirae could feel the excitement growing inside of her. Watching Tron cower away from her father the way he did right there in front of her was only the cherry on top compared to last night and the beating she gave Reese. This was all just getting to be too much.

"Sir, look," Tron said. "That's not what I was sayin'. I was just tellin' her, your daughter, that I want a DNA test or somethin' to make sure that I know if the babies is mine or if they not."

George shrugged. "Aight," he said, then smiled a crooked smile. "I ain't got no problem with that. But I'll tell you what I do have a problem with. I got a problem with you callin' my daughter out a name like that."

"My bad, Sir," Tron said. "I ain't mean it like that. I just...I ain't mean it like that."

George snickered for a hot second – a second that was not only super long for Tron, but also long for Desirae. Within the flash of an eye, George had socked Tron in his face, causing him to fall back a little bit, almost losing his balance.

"What was that, young nigga?" George asked. "You ain't talkin' all bad and shit, now, is you? What the fuck did you call my daughter?"

Desirae backed away, more toward the kitchen so she would not find herself in the middle of any blows. Furthermore, she already knew that she was not going to do a damn thing to stop it. Within a matter of seconds, Tron was angry as hell. He got his footing back and took a couple of swings at Desirae's father. Respect was totally out of the equation now. Even though he was getting up there in years, George was able to duck Tron's tries. No sooner than he felt the swoosh of air pass his face, George was in full fight mode, really giving it to Tron. It was the first time in her life that Desirae had ever seen her father actually fight. She could now see where she got her hands from – her daddy.

Tron ducked out of the way as George just wore his ass out, right there in the living room. Once the older man got a little tired of embarrassing this younger dude, he went a little easy on him. He stopped swinging, with Tron now over by the door.

"Call my daughter a hoe again and see what happens to your ass," George warned. "I'm not gon' put up with nobody disrespectin' my little girl like that," he said. "Nigga, I will fuck you up."

Tron looked at George then to Desirae, He absolutely despised her now, as blood was dripping from his nose. He knew that Desirae had invited her father to come over when he would be there helping her move and chose not to tell him. All Tron could do was shake his head, ready to leave. He pulled the apartment door open and headed out into the hallway then downstairs. "Fuckin' bitch!" Tron yelled as he got to the bottom of the steps. "Hoe!" he yelled again.

Without even thinking, George turned away from his daughter and headed out the door. He hurried down the steps and out of the apartment building, running up behind Tron. Desirae, who had to slide into her coat, was not too far behind. She quickly caught up and could see Tron and her father involved in a full-blown, grown man fist fight.

Tron finally got a few licks on her father, but they were not fast enough or hard enough. Quickly, George had jumped on Tron like it was the last thing he would ever do in his life. He socked Tron in the head so many times that he was getting dizzy and slowly falling toward the snow-covered grass on the side of the sidewalk. Tron tried to keep his balance, but this old head had been able to put up a harder fight than he would have ever imagined.

"What was that nigga?" George asked, smiling because of how proud he was of himself that he still had it in him to beat some ass. "What was that?"

Eventually, Tron had fallen to the ground. The last thing he remembered was looking up, through his blacked eyes, at George's face. George leaned down, right there in front of Desirae, and knocked Tron out with a single hard blow. As soon as his body was lying there in the snow, George looked up at his daughter as he was taking deep breaths. "Don't you ever let no nigga talk to you like that," he said. "I don't give a fuck who the motherfucka is. He won't be talkin' to me and mine like that."

Chapter 11... Afterwards

The day Desirae watched Tron get knocked the hell out by her father went pretty smoothly after the fact. Tron actually stayed knocked out, in the snow, while George helped his daughter load up the truck with her things from her apartment. When Desirae told him that it was Tron who had rented the truck and not her, he just shrugged and looked back at Tron, lying on the ground. "We not gon' worry about that, okay?"

George and Desirae went ahead and used the truck to move her stuff over to her mother's house. George drove the truck while Desirae got into her car and followed him. As she backed out of her parking spot, she looked at Tron, still lying in the snow. She knew that he had gotten just what he deserved for calling her a hoe, among other things. And she would not look back one bit and regret a single second of it.

***

Desirae wound up actually enjoying living with her mother. Surely, it was not quite the same as having a place of her own. However, her mother did keep a cooked meal on the table and a roof over her head as she swelled by the months. In August, a few weeks before Desirae was due, there was a big baby shower at her mother's house. For the first time in quite some time, she got to see many of her cousins, as well as some old friends from school that she hadn't keep up with like she used to. Some of them had children of their own, which made the event even more fun.

Tron had tried calling Desirae, but she never answered. At this point, she was perfectly content with going this alone. A week or so after her baby shower, Desirae was getting up in the middle of the night to use the bathroom. No sooner than she finished peeing and had flushed the toilet, her water broke. Almost immediately, her body and soul were overcome with so many different kinds of emotions – emotions that she just could not describe.

Labor for Desirae wound up not being as bad as she thought it would be, especially considering that she was giving birth to two babies. Her mother was right by her side the entire time, as she gave birth to two beautiful baby boys, one of which she named George, after her father, and the other she named Austin, after her uncle – the two guys who meant the most to her in her life and had never done her wrong. Furthermore, Karen was right by her daughter's side when she went downtown to register Tron for child support. Desirae knew that if she really wanted to hurt Tron, or any nigga for that matter, she needed to hit him just where it would hurt the most: in his wallet. As Desirae cradled her two baby boys in her arms, she laughed, just thinking about how their father had treated her like she was nothing. Now, she had two of his babies and was seeking child support, whether he liked it or not. It had been a long six months after seeing him knocked out by her father in broad daylight. Oh how sweet it was to get even with someone who has done you wrong – oh so sweet. Desirae learned to never give her all to a man—a man who was not going to give the same back. The next eighteen years were about to be a long, cold trip through hell for Tron. And Desirae was going to make sure of it.

CPSIA information can be obtained
at www.ICGtesting.com
Printed in the USA
LVOW13s1433070417

530034LV00007B/376/P

9 781530 772148